# THE ROAD TO FEZ

A Novel

# The Road to Fez

## Ruth Knafo Setton

COUNTERPOINT
Washington, D.C.

*Readers may find a glossary of a few*
*foreign words at the rear of the book.*

Jacket, text design and composition by Wesley B. Tanner/Passim Editions

LIBRARY OF CONGRESS CATALOGING-IN-PUBLICATION DATA

Setton, Ruth Knafo.
    The road to Fez : a novel / Ruth Knafo Setton.
        p.  cm.
    ISBN 1-58243-082-9 (alk. paper)
    1. Americans–Morocco–Fiction.  2. Jews–Morocco–Fiction.  3. Young women–Fiction.  4. Morocco–Fiction.  5. Uncles–Fiction. I. Title.
    PS3569.E845 R6 2001
    813'.6–dc21                                                          00-06443

FIRST PRINTING

COUNTERPOINT
P.O. Box 65793
Washington, D.C. 20035-5793
Counterpoint is a member of the Perseus Books Group
10 9 8 7 6 5 4 3 2 1

For

*Maurice and Rosine Knafo,*

who believed I had wings

and

*Jojo,*

who always encouraged me to fly

*They robbed me of the blackness of your eyes in*
    *the middle of the day Suleika*
*in the middle of the day they took the purity of*
    *your face away from me*
*the grace of your profile at the threshold Suleika*
*they snatched my life, my very life from me Suleika*

–Erez Bitton, "Suleika's Qasida"

# the blue door

I'm about six in the last photo taken of me before my parents and I leave Morocco for the United States. Curly brown hair pulled back in a ponytail. Tiny white dress, sturdy bare legs. Dark eyes that look questioningly at the photographer, or at the street ahead of me. A small wanderer through life, I clutch a black purse, and pause, only for an instant, on my journey. I am resolute, firmly rooted, feet in black patent leather shoes gripping the tiled outdoor corridor. My lips are dark, as if I've just eaten a plum, and traces of the juice have stained my lips. Unsmiling, confident that in a moment I will continue on my path to the future, I can afford to let the photographer freeze me. What he doesn't know, what I don't yet know, is that in another moment, my patent leather shoes will be lifted from the tiles, will dangle in the air, as I hover between two worlds—the New and the Old, belonging to neither, clinging to both.

— *Brit Lek's journal, March 27, 1969*

"DO YOU HAVE YOUR BLOOD YET?" Zahra asks me.

"I just got it. This morning." I'm out of breath, beating heavy embroidered sheets and tapestries with what looks like a tennis racket. Smashing sense into them, shaking up clouds of tiny blue motes.

"Finally!" She gives a red and yellow carpet an extra hard smack, and her rare smile breaks out–pointed black teeth framed by two gold ones. "Did you get something he wears for the spell?"

1

I hear a sound, whip my head around. Sheets and tapestries billow and blow around us. All the windows open onto the courtyard–except Gaby's. He boarded his up from the inside. And his door is locked. Zahra told me, "When he moved back here after his wife died, he sealed the window and door like a coffin."

One of his clay jars stands guard–stained the same sunset-turquoise as the door (Zahra: *to fight the evil eye*). Whenever I go by, I twist the claw-shaped iron latch, yank it down, and pull it up, but the secret catch holds it fast. Yesterday, while Zahra kept an eye on the corridor, I tried to jimmy the lock with a bobby pin and nail file. It didn't budge. What does he hide in there?

Zahra shakes the sheet in my face. I breathe in the wet sheep wool and lemon and sky, and sneeze. "I stole his– his–" I don't know how to say shaving brush in Arabic so I make stroking motions over my face.

"Face isn't good enough." She points to her breasts and belly in the cloud-gray djellabah. "It must touch his body. Like underwear."

How old is she? Age indeterminate, bird-scrawny body, thick crown of hair and eyebrows. She seems girlish–the way she moves, scrubs, cooks, and sings to herself. But when she puts on the l'tam–the white scarf covering nose, mouth, and chin–to leave the house, her eyes are ageless: unblinking black marble.

"We have to get the key to his room," I tell her.

Her eyes open wide. I know what she's thinking. We'll

2

never get it from my grandmother, Mama Ledicia, who carries the house keys on a large brass ring around her neck. She barely reaches my shoulders but is still the scariest woman I know: an ancient sibyl, with eyes even blacker than Zahra's. Centuries of demons dance behind Mama Ledicia's eyes. She never calls me by name, only "Sheba's girl" or "na'bibesk," which seems to translate as "let me carry all your pain." When she pulls my face down to hers with both hands, I feel as if I'm staring at the High Priestess or the Judge. "She sees and knows everything," Zahra told me last week. "We have to work around her."

We leave the courtyard with its shimmering black and white mosaic-tiles, and sheets and tapestries whispering their songs to the sky. Zahra says, "Get money. Meet me in the kitchen. Now that you have your blood, we can shop for the ingredients."

I run to my room—my mother's childhood room—where I dig out some coins and large pastel bills, glancing up every second to make sure I'm not being watched. I lean on the carved window and look around the courtyard. Yellow mimosa blossoms sway gently in the breeze. The intricately designed tiles glisten under pale sun. I'm in another country, one with no signs or maps, but one I know intimately, with every pore. I listen for the hum: electric, throbbing, insistent, prickling my flesh, insinuating its way through my veins. But it only comes at night. There is so much I wish I could ask my mother, so much I don't understand. I want to ask her if she ever heard the hum. I want to ask her more about Suleika, what exactly she wants me to do. Light a candle at her grave in Fez? Write her story? And Gaby. What would Mom feel if she knew what's happening to me? Maybe she is here, watching me fall in love with her younger brother.

I check on the bits and pieces of Gaby I've collected over the past month, since I've been in Morocco. Hidden on the shelf behind Camus' *Essais Lyriques* and Proust's *Un Amour de Swann* (I trust that they were men of secrets themselves, who won't give me away). A pitiful showing, but as Zahra tells me: *Gaby knows spells, he leaves no clues.* Two empty Gitane boxes, still smelling strongly of tobacco, the black gypsy dancing against blue desert sky. Three small wood matchboxes, decorated with a painted camel, a vintage car, a palm tree. The ivory-handled shaving brush, its bristles a pale, gleaming gold, like the Pennsylvania fields of corn I used to ride my bike past every fall. At night I stroke the soft bristles over my face and throat, pretend they are his hands.

In the kitchen Zahra waits for me impatiently. "Come on. We have to hurry." She stashes the money into a tiny black velvet pouch worn around her throat, then kneels behind the kitchen staircase and opens a small cupboard. She brings out her spare djellabah, a soft gray—identical to the one she's wearing—and a white l'tam. She stands and rolls the scarf and djellabah into a ball that she crushes beneath her arm.

We move quietly through the house and back outside, where we run to the mellah gate, locked every night until recently. The arched stone gate of the Jewish quarter that my Uncle Haim swears kept Jews safe from a mad Sultan or a rampaging mob, but that Gaby swears—with equal vehemence—made us targets, closed in a world with no way out.

In the shadows behind the arch, I pull the djellabah down over my head and breathe Zahra's cumin and burnt leaf scent. It's too short and narrow, snug across my hips. Zahra covers my nose and mouth with the l'tam and ties the ends behind my head. She folds the hood of the djellabah down low over my forehead so that all you can see of my face are my eyes. I push the flaps of the hood back behind my ears so it will stay in place and not flop forward.

We leave the mellah and merge with the stream of people walking up and down the rue Moulay-Youssef. Clouds of dust blow in my eyes. Squinting, I pass women in creamy haiks, one dark eye exposed, high heels peeking out from under. I try to walk quickly the way they do, but the veil and long gown get in my way. Carefully, I place one foot in front of the other, as if I've never walked down this street before. As if my dad didn't ride his bike up this hill (*We were so poor my brother and I shared one bike, each using one pedal*), as if Mom and her sisters didn't giggle here, sharing longings and gossip, right here, on the cobblestones. I am breathing so hard that my nostrils press the l'tam in and out.

A hand grabs my shoulder. I jerk around and see a man in a business suit staring at me with sharp eyes, as if he can see through my disguise. He speaks rapid Arabic in a very deep voice. I can't understand a word he says. "A Sidi, ana m'juja," I mumble and run past him, hoping he won't chase me to ask where my husband is.

Instead of continuing down the rue Moulay-Youssef to the Bab Sha'aba, the gate that opens onto the sophisticated Place de France–with its cafes and shops and Modes de Paris, the boutique managed by Sylvie, Gaby's official girl-friend–we turn right, into the narrow entrance to the me-dina. I take a deep breath. A lifetime of fear clouds my eyes. The very first words Mama Ledicia said to me when I ar-rived in El Kajda: "Don't go in the medina. Jews go there and disappear. Janine who went to meet the Arab boy she liked. Never seen again. And Laurette. Same thing. Disap-peared. And Suleika. She entered the Arab world, and we all know what happened to her." She slit her throat with her stubby finger.

And Dad left me at the airport with a string of warnings, wound as tightly around me as the wool scarf knotted around his throat: "Be invisible. Remember my brother. Knifed in the back when he left a Jewish meeting. And my cousin, Pinoche. Your mother's Uncle Sollie. Don't look any-one in the eye. Don't draw attention to yourself. Don't talk too much or too loudly. Don't go alone to the medina or the port. Don't go anywhere at night, unless you're with Haim or Gaby. Remember, you have two things working against you: you're a Jew and a woman."

Zahra tugs me by the arm. I take a deep breath behind the veil and follow her into the medina. We enter the spice mer-chant's small booth. Za'atar: pungent green powder. Cumin:

6

harsh, biting through my nostrils. While she shops, I dig my hands into burlap bags of spices: cinnamon, cloves, cumin, saffron–running the grains up and down my arms. My wrists tingle. I wish the veil covered them as well.

We leave the spice merchant and go down a narrow cobblestone alley. Blinded by the veil and the pyramid of tumbling packages in my arms, I bump into the earth-colored water carrier, copper cups and goatskin twined on leather cords around his neck and waist. Vendors insist–in rhyming chants–that we bite into figs purple and green, or smell the vast stalks of fragrant mint leaves, luisa, sheba.

We stop at another merchant who sells cosmetics. Zahra buys green henna, adding the twine-wrapped parcel to the others I am holding. As I follow her down the street–past tiny cafes and booths, veiled women carrying enormous baskets, hooded merchants staring at us–I feel numb, as if I'm doing what was written for me centuries ago. Walking through the seething medina at this exact instant. Disguised as an Arab. Preparing a spell. Even loving Gaby. I have never felt less free.

IN AN ATTEMPT TO FIGURE OUT HOW TO GET THE KEY to his room from Mama Ledicia, I trail after the women of the family, the way I used to trail after Mom to tell her about my day at school and my dreams and fears. *Read,* she told me, *keep learning about the outside world. Don't worry about housework, you can pick that up later.* I feel like a trespasser in their world, always a beat too slow and clumsy. Zahra covers for me, helps me with all the heavy tasks, while we eye the brass key ring and exchange desperate looks.

Perla winds a white turban around my head, like hers, and grins at me. "Ah Brit, I'm so glad you're here." My favorite aunt, my cousin Mani's mother, she glows with restless vitality. I love everything about her: her crazy sense of humor, the slight mustache above her dimpled smile, the tufts of henna-orange rooster hair sticking up from her head, the way she rubs her nose with the back of her wrist and wiggles her big rear end in tight black pants. Her husband, Simon, died last year in a car accident. Although Perla doesn't possess Gaby's and my mother's dark-gold desert beauty, Mani tells me that every unmarried man over thirty in El Kajda is after her. She hugs me close. I smell her anise-scented breath as she whispers, "Be strong, chérie. Sheba's watching you. I feel her near."

Helping Zahra, my grandmother, and aunts with the Pesach cleaning, I discover that every room has secrets. Hidden truths surface as we pull open mattresses and take out the stuffing of sheep wool, washing it by hand until it is soft as silk. The small mirror face-down inside my Aunt Perla's mattress. *A contraceptive*, whispers Zahra. A silver knife under pregnant Mamouche's mattress. Zahra: *to pray for a boy child*. The tiny black velvet sacks filled with herbs that Mamouche's kids attach to their underclothes. *To guard against the evil eye*, explains Zahra. Djnoun hover everywhere, grasp secrets and use them against us.

"You know how to deal with djnoun, don't you?" Gaby asked me that day, that endless, unforgettable day four years ago–March 18, 1965–when he came from his ship to visit us in Horsens. He smelled of sea and salt, a pirate blown to America on a spice wind. We stood on the corner of Candlestick and Wise, between my parents' apartment building and Mrs. Kopf's, staring at her window. The curtain moved slightly. "See?" I cried. "She's always spying on me!"

He watched quietly, then said, "Get me some salt."

I ran inside, past my parents in the living room, grabbed the blue and white salt container with the girl under an umbrella, raced back out, and handed it to him.

"What's this djinn's name? Kop?"

"Kopf."

He nodded and poured the salt in a circle on the cracked sidewalk in front of her apartment. He chanted in Arabic. I caught the name "Kopf." The curtain was completely still. She was watching. I felt her evil gaze burn through the glass and cloth. He scattered more salt, muttered a few words he made me repeat. He shook the salt over his left shoulder. Then he set the container in the center of the salt circle. Rubbed his hands together. "There, my cat. She won't bother you again."

Turbaned and wrapped in a white apron, I dust the salon arabe in my grandparents' house, a stranglehold of memory–from the wall of old photos to Gaby's ceramic vessels: at least four feet high, red-stained sentinels from an ancient desert palace, guarding each corner. But the heart of the room is the long brass key that hangs in the center of a white wall. When I first saw the key, with a wall to itself, as if it held the answer to every mystery, I thought it was Gaby's key–miraculously out in the open, like Poe's purloined letter, where no one would think to look. But one night after dinner, when we all sauntered into this room for mint tea and sweets, Papa Naphtali told us a story about our old house in Toledo, with its orange trees and blue-tiled walls, and he pointed to the key and said, "One day we'll return home." Later, Perla explained that he was talking about our family's house in Spain, when our ancestors fled the Inquisition by sailing across the Strait of Gibraltar to Morocco. But he had described the scent of orange blossoms and the courtyard where we drank wine and watched the moon so vividly and fondly that it seemed as if we had just left Spain yesterday.

I stare at the brass key now, gleaming yet forlorn on its wall, and think of Gaby's key, and the key to the mellah gate: somehow all related, as if they are all the same key, but I can't find the link to unlock the door.

Dusting my way through time, I see a photo of my mother at my age, pregnant with me, laughing with arms outstretched. A photo of Tonton Elie and Gaby as boys, which Perla calls "The Sacred and the Profane": Elie, pale and solemn, next to taller Gaby, who squints into the sun, holding a cat in his arms. I even find myself nearly unrecognizable, sitting on my mother's lap, in a wide-sleeved gold caftan, my curls slicked down, my expression as disagreeable as ever. Next to me, with a hopeful, open smile, sits Mani on Perla's lap–before the fever hit, dark curls as loose and glowing as Gaby's, tumbling around his face.

The old man, Rabbi Abraham ben Avram, our saint-ancestor, glares at me. Papa Naphtali told me about his hiloula: the night of miracles held at his shrine on the outskirts of El Kajda, seventeen days after Pesach. It is like a wedding between God and human beings, with the saint as the matchmaker. His spirit returns, and he listens to our prayers and carries them back to God. Papy told me that Rabbi Abraham was known for performing many miracles. A mystic who talked to animals and turned himself invisible, he flew like a bird when he had to prevent a disaster. Once he even stopped time, just to save a little boy. He looked at you and knew in a moment if you told the truth or not. He touched you, and you were cured of whatever ailed you. At dawn he talked to God. At night he sang in his courtyard, and everyone came to listen. They gathered outside, under the fig tree, and he sang to them of God and miracles and hope. You listened and you cried. When the music stopped, you still heard his oud, his voice vibrating through the sky.

Rabbi Abraham's ferocious black eyes follow me through the room, penetrate me, and find me wanting. Perla told me that when they were kids, Gaby covered the saint's eyes with a postcard of the Wicked Witch of the West, and it was a week before Mamouche tattled to Papy, and he got punished.

To hide from Rabbi Abraham's eyes, I crouch and peer through my favorite of Gaby's vessels. It burns with a hidden

11

light, like a moon in the corner of the room. On my knees, I discover a mirror glued to the inside wall that sends rays shooting back through openings in the clay. I feel as if I'm peering through the keyhole into Gaby's soul.

THAT NIGHT MANI AND I GO TO THE MAJESTIC, where we hook up with Jacky, Luc, Isabelle, and Mani's few remaining friends who haven't left for Paris or Lucerne. We dance for hours on a hot, tiny red-lit floor, to Mani's idol, James Brown, and Otis Redding and Wilson Pickett. Afterward, under midnight sky, we walk along the beach to the Café Tamarik, where I order my favorite, kehouwa me'hersa, literally "broken coffee," coffee and milk swirled and foamed together. I love the sound of the words on my tongue, and even more, the image of coffee broken with milk. Here, all languages are broken, colliding: Arabic, Judeo-Arabic, Berber dialects, French, Spanish, Ladino, English. We speak in slivers and fragments, pieces of a puzzle that will never fit. As we say a word, its meaning shifts: no becomes yes, and yes is usually no. We whisper, especially people's names. Words from the heart are unspoken; half-finished sentences drift into a hush. The evil eye watches. We are never alone. Women's tongues are sharp, but only in their domain–the rooftop, courtyard and kitchen, where they dissect an entire town and then sew it back together. Men speak quietly, their eyes darting and watchful. Greenblack leaves tremble with the weight of eyes and voices. Mama Ledicia told me: *A man may wear a white djellabah and be filthy inside. He may carry a knife behind his back and smile.*

Is this what the converso existence is like—when one sus-
pects everyone of being a spy, when revealing one's true self
can mean death? But I wonder: were Dad, Mom and I freer
in America? I think we were even more afraid, hiding behind our disguise: three newly minted Christians from Paris,
sprouted from nowhere. I thought we were rootless. I forgot
we'd ever had a home.

I picture Dad at the airport: smaller and frailer than I'd
ever seen him—as if he were shrinking since Mom died.
Dark glasses, as always, masked his eyes. Suddenly I
couldn't listen to his warnings, or even look at him for another second. I turned and ran to the plane. Staring out the
window, I imagined him already back in the silent apartment, the black and gold globe of the world finally still. Like
Mom. Like my heart. Not even a flutter. I kept seeing her
hands smoothing over the layers of wallpaper and hearing
her voice singing me to sleep, "Le rêve bleu" the song she
always sang when I woke up from bad dreams: Léger,
mystérieux / Comme un oiseau / S'envolant dans les cieux. I
tried to keep her there, safe in the blue dream, far from pain
and memory. But she clicked her teeth against her tongue,
the way she did when I exasperated her, and I ran and ran
from the sound, even though my feet were locked under the
seat before me and the seat belt held me firmly in place. The
blue dream surrounded me. Her song, the sound of her teeth
clicking against my tongue, the way her childhood dream of
a blue man had entered my dreams when I was a girl—until I

forgot whose dream it had been first. He was all blue, she told me, head to toe, and he came through my window when I was growing up, long before I met your father.

When she'd told me about the blue man in Horsens, our hometown in Pennsylvania, I didn't understand how a man—even a blue man—could enter a window, but here, in El Kajda, when I stood at the window of her childhood room, I saw how easy it would be for a man, for anyone, to enter the tiny room, no larger than a closet. The window was nothing but a hole punched through the stucco wall. No screen or glass, no blinds, nothing to provide privacy, open to the inner courtyard and the sweet smell of the mimosa tree. I leaned on the window—more a circle than a square—and waited for the blue man to enter. He'd entered my dreams in Horsens—and there, the window had been protected by glass, blinds, curtain. Every night for a week after I arrived in El Kajda, I waited for him. And then, on the seventh night, I heard the hum for the first time. And on the eighth morning I woke up and saw Gaby leaning in my window, smiling at me.

THE NEXT DAY, AFTER A FRANTIC, WHISPERED DISCUSSION with Zahra, I offer to do the laundry. Without a word, Mama Ledicia pulls me down the hall to Gaby's blue door. I tremble, being so near the forbidden place. She narrows her eyes and mutters in Arabic, "Do you think I was born yesterday? Sheba's girl, he's not for you. You will not put a spell on him!"

I'm nearly crouching, staring at her. I don't even attempt to lie to those knowing eyes. "Because he's my uncle?"

She stands on tiptoe and fixes me with eyes like black fire. "In old times girls married their uncles or cousins. And had sick babies. Now and then a primitive family still does it. But not this family. And definitely not this girl. Or this uncle."

"Why not?"

"Because of who he is—married to his vision of clay. And because of who you are—married to your vision of him. You'll always want more than he can give."

"I have other dreams! I want to write, to travel, to—"

"Do it, na'bibesk. Your mother wanted you to go to Suleika in Fez. Go! Much as I love having you here, you're in danger."

"Stop it, Mamy! You're starting to scare me."

She shakes her head. "You're eighteen, but in this world you're a child, playing with things you don't understand. And you have no mother to watch over you. I have to do it."

"Papa Naphtali says that—"

She dismisses her husband's words with a wave of her hand. "What do men know? Nothing. They sit on the roof or do business in the street. They don't understand any of the important things that happen, the true way life works. Listen to me. Follow your mother's wishes and go to Fez. Pray to Suleika. You need to be strong." She presses her fingertips against my forehead and blesses me in Arabic. I lower my eyes and pretend to accept—but inside, I'm furious. Yes, Mama Ledicia, I'm definitely going to ask Suleika for advice. A girl who chose death over life, who knew nothing about love, who—in Mom's words—welcomed death with open arms because she thought it was her chance to meet up with God. Everyone thinks they know what's best for me. I'll find my own way to get the key.

IN THE COURTYARD, I LEAN AGAINST PERLA'S LEGS and half-heartedly help the women prepare for the Pesach seder. I sift through grains of rice. Like my mother's, their hands are never still. They sort legumes, scrape carrots, mash garlic cloves, slice beets, pare apples, and squeeze oranges for sweet jam. Zahra sweeps the black and white mosaic-tiles with long languorous glides that make her look as if she's skating. The mimosa tree is motionless at noon; not until night does it start trembling, long yellow pom-pom branches brushing against the floor. The courtyard is roofless, a secret world invisible from the street. Like the riad, an enclosed garden in a house. Or the mellah behind the arched gate, an intimate world turned in on itself.

Pregnant Mamouche, the sister between Perla and my mother, reminds me of the White Rabbit, always frazzled and harried, nostrils red and scraped. Her nose twitches and eyes tear, even though Perla is the one chopping onions. Long needles fly over Mamouche's belly as she knits a pale yellow blanket for her third child, due in about a month, at the end of April. She's married to dark, volatile Haim, who dwarfs and dominates her. With a sly glance at Perla, she begins the daily soap opera: "Samy Sasportas is back in town. I saw him in the Place de France, wearing a brown robe with a gold cross swinging over his chest."

16

Perla makes a rude sound. "Do you remember when Samy Sasportas turned religious and chased kids through town, scaring them half to death, screaming that the Messiah was on his way?"

"M'skina, his poor mother," says Mama Ledicia. I smell the juice of oranges from the jam she is making. Long white apron tied around her, she sits on a low stool, her feet not quite reaching the tiles. A dark blue kerchief covers the cloud of gray crackling hair–her secret. In the privacy of her room, she bends forward and brushes the waist-length mass from beneath. Once I watched from the doorway and ran when she raised her head: I knew I had eavesdropped on an intimate act.

Perla says, "Remember when he tried to slice off Voleur's ear?"

Mama Ledicia frowns. "I never let him play with Gaby after that day."

Justine, smoking a small, thin cigar, says coolly: "So? Samy Sasportas tortures cats, Gaby tortures women. It's only a matter of degree." An old school friend of Perla's, Justine is divorced, a photographer who lives in Paris and returns often for visits. Short and slender, with a glossy cap of black hair, she dresses in men's clothes, often with suspenders, embroidered vest, narrow silk tie.

Mamouche nods. "That's true. Haim says he had the perfect woman–"

"Not Estrella, God rest her soul!" cries Perla.

"There was something wrong with that poor girl," says

17

Mama Ledicia, swiftly peeling and slicing oranges, dropping them into a bucket at her side.

"Wild eyes," says Justine.

I remember Mom and I studying the photo Gaby had sent us two years ago, right after his wedding, with a note scribbled in French on a torn sheet of newspaper. We squinted to decipher his writing over the newsprint. Finally, what we had was this: *Sheba, my delicious cabbage, I'm caught. Here she is. Is it too late to fly to you? I kiss your wings. She is terrified of my love for you. I am in someone's hands. I hope not God's.*

We examined the photo hungrily. The newlyweds stood under the wide, flat leaves of a palm tree. Faces latticed and scrolled with shadows. He frowned at us, with dark wounded mouth, while she—undeniably beautiful, with long coils of black hair—smiled pleadingly at him.

Mamouche twitches her nose. "Haim insists she was the perfect woman."

"Haim." Perla makes that rude sound again, deep in her throat. "Funny how even when he's not here, he still manages to get in the conversation." She rubs her eyes, tearing now from the onions. Even I feel the burning in my eyes.

"How did she die?" I ask.

Mamouche gasps and pinches her nostrils as if I've said something horrifying. Mama Ledicia clicks her teeth against her tongue, reminding me of Mom. I turn back to look at Perla. Her eyes—usually so direct—are focused somewhere beyond me. Maybe at Gaby's boarded-up window. A blackbird lands on a branch of the mimosa tree, clinging to the yellow pom-pom blossoms. Sun glints across the tiles. I turn back and watch as Justine flicks ashes into her empty tea glass. She squints, red lips pursed, as if staring at me through a camera eye. Finally she says, "No secret, ma petite. He did it."

"Aa'wili!" cries Mama Ledicia, rocking back and forth. "Don't say such things!"

"How?" I breathe.

"Be fair, Justine! Not with his hands," says Perla.

"No—" Justine shakes her head almost regretfully. "Just by being himself, poor bastard."

Mama Ledicia shakes her head disapprovingly. "Justine, you go too far. It wasn't his fault. You don't know the whole story. What Gaby needs is to find the right woman."

"Excuse me, Mama Ledicia, but there is no right woman for a man like that."

"Justine is immune." Perla gives her a satisfied, almost admiring look.

"Not exactly," says Justine. "I'm not immune to beauty— male or female. I wish he'd let me photograph him. I've been asking him for years. But it's not that. In Paris, there are a hundred Gaby's, a thousand, an army of crowing cocks. Only there, no one listens. What I truly feel for him is a sort of envy. How does he manage to work at the sardine factory, survive in this country, and still get inspired to create at the pôterie? I had to leave Morocco to become a photographer. I was suffocating here."

I watch Justine closely. Is she playing the same game I am, trying to hide her true feelings? Can she be as wise and free as she sounds? Oh, Big Sister, if it is true that you are immune, then maybe I can absorb some of your strength.

"You're a woman," Perla reminds her. "Gaby has more freedom. He goes wherever he likes."

"Where he's not supposed to," says Mamouche. "Haim says—"

Perla snorts. Mamouche glares at her, but stops what she was about to say.

Justine taps ashes into the small glass. "I ran into Sylvie at the Café Tamarik yesterday, and she told me that she and Gaby are getting married in June. She's already ordered her wedding gown from Paris."

Perla mutters a sharp burst of words in Arabic that signals a joke and the wild bursts of laughter that inevitably follow: my grandmother's throaty cackle, Perla's raucous horse neigh, Mamouche's breathless giggle, and Justine's delighted, low laugh. Encouraged, Perla starts in on another joke in Arabic. Even when they tell jokes in French, they always switch to Arabic for the punch line—which means I always need a translation. They puzzle over it with good intentions, but finally tell me: it can't be translated.

I'm not surprised. I'm trying to translate something myself here. Take a girl from one world. Set her in an alien world for many years, but make sure she takes along a fragment with her, something that can never be stolen. A smell. A cloud of tart-sweet memory that assures she will never forget. Bring Gaby, the originator of the cloud, to confront her in the faraway land, thereby creating new configurations and combinations. He stands in that land, a man trapped between two times, two worlds. He looks lost, drowning in the sea between them, but he smiles with his eyes and laughs fiercely, explosively, with his whole body—and nobody but the girl sees how lost he is. After one night he disappears again and goes back to his world. And now four years later, she returns to the old world. They're all here, the ones she left behind. Even *she* is here, the little girl she'd abandoned in this memory-house. But she enters like a visitor from another planet, one who remembers everything and understands nothing, and who must translate the forgotten language for him.

I GET UP TO LEAVE BUT MAMOUCHE, STILL SNIFFING, points her knitting needle at me. "Women smell. Do you hear me, Brita?"

"What?" I say, startled, and everyone laughs.

"Je suis franche. I can't lie. Now that Sheba's gone, may she rest in peace, and you're of marrying age, we need to help you. No one talks about this, but it's something every girl needs to know. We smell, and we have to wash—more than other women."

"Speak for yourself," says Perla.

"You can fight it all you want. We marocaines need to scrub and scrub."

"Take notes, Brit," mutters Justine.

I laugh, and Mamouche points the needle at me again. The needle is huge, glittering, silver. I imagine it flying through the air and slicing off my head in a clean stroke. Like Suleika's. A Jew and a woman, as Dad said. Throats have been slit for less.

"You think it's funny," says Mamouche, "because you were raised in America. But you can't escape it. It's your blood. It's you. You have to wash at least twice a day. *There.* Where it counts."

"Personally, I like the smell of women," says Justine, studying her cigar.

"Don't listen to her," Mamouche says seriously. "What we like doesn't matter. It doesn't change anything. You have to wash. You have to scrub."

"When will I ever be clean enough?" I ask Mamouche, only half joking. Turning back, I stare at my window as if I'll see Mom looking out at me.

*In our search for Lalla Aziza,* the notorious Witch of Fez, whose love-philtres had enchanted half the city, the boy Abdullah and I stumbled onto the Square Bab-Dekaken, where reigned a scene of utter horror. A ferocious, gesticulating crowd, gripped by a violent fever, spilled over the edge of the square—a flood of humanity in this desert kingdom. Moors in green and white turbans brandished sabers and spurred their Arabian steeds, scattering clouds of red dust. Jews in black skullcaps, pathetic creatures with anguished eyes, wailed a name over and over: "Suleika!" Voices were raised in shouts and cries. The stench of sweat was suffocating.

Abdullah had disappeared, but he was like a small playful monkey, exploring whatever caught his fancy. I knew that he would return momentarily, yet my heart beat fast. I felt the fury of the crowd directed against me. Whilst I wore the loose flowing djellabah favored by the women of this tradition-bound Moorish Society, I smoked a small pipe stacked with my favorite cherry tobacco, and I refused to cover my face. I had not voyaged halfway around the world in order to be hampered by a muslin cloth that obstructed my breathing and blocked my vision. I suddenly recalled my father's words when I left England: "You are not, nor will you ever be, a true woman!"

An old woman at my side made a trilling sound so piercing it unsteadied me. I nearly fell against a tall man wearing a deep scarlet burnoose. With a muttered imprecation, he pushed me away roughly. Despite my uneasiness, I asked him in rudimentary Arabic about the cause of the din and commotion. His large eyes blazed with rage, "A stained girl!" he shouted. "She deserves death!"

"What did she do?" I asked.

His eyes swept over me, his dark face contorting with scorn and loathing.

*"A man-woman. Like you! Going where men go. No modesty!" He stopped abruptly and spit in my face.*

*I felt it on my cheek but did not touch it or look away. I had never before been confronted with such pure hatred.*

*I tried to move, but the mass of people formed a wall of heads, shoulders, backs, and elbows. They shouted and cursed, fists flailing at the sky. Who was Suleika? What sin was so unforgivable that she could only pay for it with her life?*

*Loud rifle cracks like thunder exploded through the square. A woman screamed in my ear, "She is dead! Allah be praised! Now we are safe!"*

*The women trilled their jubilation, a jungle of shrill, bloodthirsty magpies. People leaped into the air, hugged and shouted with laughter.*

*There was no air. I forgot why I was in this cursed square, why I had ever come to this kingdom of savagery and blood-lust, why I had insisted on seeing what hid behind the veil of civilization . . .*

—Lady Theodora Bird,
*Wings of a Bird:*
*Memoirs of a Lady Traveller in*
*North Africa, 1832–1839*

# *trespasser*

THE DAY BEFORE EREV PESACH. Only twenty-four hours until the end of my period. And Zahra and I are no closer to getting Gaby's key, or his underwear. When Lydia, the new teacher from Algeria, asks me to go to the port with her, I don't hesitate. It means seeing him—and who knows? Maybe I can lift his key without him noticing.

We drive in her green Renault past low-swooping clouds of seagulls, large open trucks, a row of cafés facing the water, fishermen unloading their cargo of sardines—glistening silver, mouths gaping—into large buckets. Lydia thinks I don't see through her, that I don't wonder at this twenty-six-year-old woman's sudden friendship. She holds my hand as she drives, admires my long Indian cotton skirt, tells me she's dying to coil my wild curls into a sleek French twist, but insists I need to lose the sandals: "Toes are the ugliest part of a woman's body. The wisest thing to do is to hide them."

"But men have toes too."

She laughs. "Ah, you Americans. So literal. Of course men have toes, but they are clever enough to keep them hidden.

We'll go shopping next week, and I'll help you choose a lovely pair of shoes, the kind that makes a man think you don't walk—you *float*."

How tempting to believe she's my friend. But my aunts' warnings stay with me. Perla: *It was hell growing up as his sister. One false friend after another. Dropping me as soon as they got to him.* And Mamouche: *I used to lie for him. I'd stand at the door and say he wasn't home, while he ran upstairs to the roof and escaped, leaping from roof to roof, until he was out of the mellah.*

The Afriat sardine factory, a square beige building, is the first in a line of factories at the port. Lydia points out the small cottage behind the factory, where Gaby and his wife used to live. A gingerbread cottage, like Hansel and Gretel's: yellow, with an arched green door. "An Arab family lives there now," she tells me, "but it's like a tourist site. As soon as I arrived, one of the other teachers showed it to me and told me that after Gaby's wife died, he brought a different woman here every night for six months."

The smell of fresh fish is overpowering, dizzying, as we climb the factory steps. From the moment I open the enormous clanging iron doors, I know I've made a mistake coming here, as if I'm nothing more than one of his groupies, tracking him down at work. He looks at us, upper lip curling in complete scorn. My cousin Mani shakes his head at me. And my uncle Haim starts yelling.

After a minute of staring down at the blazing red furnace, the rows of kerchiefed Arab women packing sardines in tins, the men of my family watching me with contempt, I turn and leave, letting the heavy doors slam shut behind me. I breathe in the biting salt air and watch fishermen load the boats–grass green, blood-orange, egg-yellow, turquoise. I know why Gaby treats me like a child. Mama Ledicia is right: even at eighteen, I am stupid in life. I don't understand how it works, the movement behind the scenes. My child-hood in Pennsylvania, my dreams of adventure and glory, my escape into books and drugs, even my boyfriend, Sun God–nothing prepared me for this world of evasion, secrecy, and oblique quarter-truths.

The door opens behind me. I hear the roar, the machine hum and whir, before the door slams. I smell Lydia's per-fume: Shalimar. Syrup-clinging. I will always associate this swamp-thick scent with the factory, Gaby's curled lip, the bobbing boats, the fire-hell of my own ignorance.

Lydia's eyes are bright, hard. "There's nothing sexier than a desperate man, one who's at the edge and doesn't care anymore. Your uncle Gaby is a gorgeous wreck."

"What do you want from him?"

"The same thing you do, chérie. And every other woman in town." Her laugh cuts through the clotted gray air. "Smile, little one. I arranged everything. We're meeting the men for lunch."

Half an hour later we enter a dark red and green café, doors open wide, facing the boats and the water. Inside, it is crowded with fishermen seated at small white tables. Lydia and I push two round tables together and sit, side by side, facing the water, the boats, the sun. Salt breezes blow the triangular wax napkins to the floor.

A navy fisherman's cap tilted back on his head, Gaby smokes and laughs with a group of men at the entrance. He doesn't look at us.

Mani glides like a pale fish between the tables, kisses me on the cheek, and whispers, "Idiot! This isn't the way to get him!"

A glowering bear, Haim doesn't pause to greet anyone, starting in on me right away, even before he sits. "What are you doing here? What was Sheba thinking? She didn't teach you where you belong, how to cook or clean, how to take care of children. Go to Mamouche. She'll teach you to be a lady."

Gaby comes up behind him, leans over the table, and kisses my cheeks. "Little cat. And Lydia. Welcome to the port."

"Look around," says Haim, eyes still fixed on me. "There are no Jews here but us. No women but you two. And no Jewish women but you, Brit. Sheba should have taught you—"

"Shut up about my mother!"

Haim's eyes goggle, and he leans over the table as if he's going to punch me, but Lydia murmurs, "What's wrong with being the only women? Less competition that way." Her normally loud, high-pitched voice is changed. She sounds as if she's been running. She smiles at Gaby—with teeth. I've never been face to face with this kind of hunger. I'm repelled—and fascinated. Wish I had the courage to bare myself so openly. To grab him by the soul and say: somewhere, somehow, you're mine. A mistake has been made. They call you my uncle. You can't be. It's impossible. You see it, don't you? You feel it too—don't you?

His back is to me as he pulls a chair between Lydia and me, and I know he's feeling her, the same tug of desire I'm feeling. She's screaming it with her red lips and big teeth. I stare at the back of his faded black tee-shirt. Wrinkled. A hole in the right sleeve, just off the shoulder. The back of his neck covered by loose black curls. Only a glint of skin—light, almost pale—compared to the gold-dark arm gesturing as he talks to her. The other arm stretched over the back of her chair.

He sits back in his chair when the waiter arrives. Tall and thin, with frizzy black hair pulled back in a tiny ponytail. The waiter smiles, showing three gold teeth, and shifts the round copper tray balanced against his narrow hip. "Gaby, la'bass?"

"La'bass, Mohammed. Kul sheeb'kher?"

"L'hamdou lilla," Mohammed replies.

Lydia laughs loudly as if he said something funny, then says, "You order for me, Gaby."

He turns to me briefly. "I'll order for you too."

I'm focused on my hands. The way the fingers branch out from the palm. The almost excruciating sensuality of our nearly webbed fingers. And toes. We're like ducks, birds, animals. Beasts, beneath the voices and clothes and masks. Haim, preaching his stale morality. Even pale feverish Mani,

29

moving his head to music only he hears. And Gaby and Lydia at my side. Beasts, already gnawing at each other. A red clammy smell fills my nostrils. More than her Shalimar, the salt of the sea, the smoke of their cigarettes, the sardines.

Mani kicks my leg. Hard. Twice. I lift my eyes from my obscenely joined fingers groping at each other, trying to create a tent of safety to hide behind, and see him framed by the open doors, waves sucking and biting the boats. Tata Perla's only son—his father Simon died last year in a car accident—he's nineteen, my closest friend. Like Zahra, my accomplice. He spies on Gaby at the factory and the Majestic for me. He shakes his head again, unconscious of the slipping wig. An attack of rheumatic fever at eight left him hairless. Everywhere. No eyebrows or lashes. Without his wig, he looks like an egg: luminous, eerie. The wig—a coarse, shaggy brown Beatle cut—refuses to stay glued to his head, constantly tips over his eyebrow, then flies off, especially when he dances. His wig reminds me of the falsies I wore briefly in high school that kept falling out of my bra. Once landing on my shoe as I talked to Tony Galetti, the most popular guy in school.

Mani pencils in eyebrows to make himself appear more natural, but they give him a surreal Marlene Dietrich look. To cover his lashless eyes, he often wears dark glasses—like my father. But when he takes them off, and you adjust to the pallor and hairlessness of his face, you see that his eyes are extraordinary, a rich molasses-brown. "Muddy," he says, but they're not: they're dark as the woods. His smile is lopsided, adorable. He's tall and thin like me, slouched like me. Both of us feel too tall, too thin.

"My friend Luc's been asking about you," Mani says. His arched brows and wig look incongruous in this café of swarthy, macho fishermen. "I didn't have to leave home to be an exile," he told me once. "No matter how hard it was for you, it was worse for me. At least, you're beautiful."

"No, I'm not," I protested. "I've got a ball on the tip of my nose. And it's too big. And I have frog eyes. And my upper lip is bigger than my lower lip."

"True. By all rights, you shouldn't be beautiful. The pieces aren't perfect. They don't really fit together. But somehow when you put it all together, you get . . . Brit. Like no one else."

My eyes blink wet as I remember, and I wish I could reach across the table and hug him. I trust him implicitly. He is brutally honest–with me, as well as with himself–the only person I believe without any reservations. He's been hurt too much in his life to play games with truth. The scapegoat of every kid game, school an absolute torture, boys jeering at him, girls ignoring him, he cuts to the heart of every matter, with no forced sentimentality, no fear.

He leans toward me. "We'll go dancing tonight. At the Majestic. D'accord?"

I nod. Words can't exit my mouth. Not yet. I'm undergoing a strange metamorphosis. More than the webbed animal hands. My teeth are sharpening, cutting through my cheeks. I want to bite. To devour. To slash and kill. Lydia? Or Gaby?

31

Mohammed, an exception to the strict male/female roles–like Mani, like me–minces exaggeratedly toward us, as if he's wearing spike heels. He reminds me of Sylvie. Gold teeth glittering, he sets down brown bottles of ale, with glasses for Lydia and me, and two loaves of round bread, a dish of tomato and onion salad, a small bowl of black olives. A moment later, he returns with heaping plates of steaming whole sardines. An empty tray against his hip, he bends over Gaby's neck. Breathes in.

I'm watching, snorting fire. Not missing a thing. The Beast waits for the moment to attack. Lydia leans over and watches Gaby rip apart a sardine with long tobacco-stained fingers and bite into the tender flesh. She rubs her throat as though he were biting into her neck.

I drink ale from the bottle–to Haim's disapproving glance–and pick up a whole sardine with my fingers. Burning hot. I drop it on the wax napkin, then take it up again, separate the meat from the skeleton, and bite delicately–no, I'm *not* a Beast. Tastes of sea and sun. Grilled and seasoned with lemon, garlic and olive oil. I wash it down with ice-cold brown ale, and pick up another sardine. Grateful to use my hunger on food, to keep my groping hands busy.

Gaby turns and says accusingly, "You left the best parts. Near the head and tail." He picks up my abandoned sardine, shakes it in my face, and says, "Eat."

I look into his eyes. More yellow than green. The way I imagine wolf eyes. No gentleness. No forgiveness. Cold eyes. He pushes the sardine against my mouth. I take a small bite.

My teeth graze his index finger. He shudders. Or is it me? "Do you like it?" he asks. He sounds mocking, as cold as his eyes. "You'll never taste fresher sardines. Caught this morning."

Mani says loudly, "So Brit, we're going to the Majestic tonight. Luc really likes you. He's from Paris. His father works at the Mairie."

"A very rich family," says Lydia. "You could do a lot worse, ma petite."

Gaby nearly shoves the sardine into my mouth. I can't look away from his eyes. The second he turns back to Lydia, I choke. Drink ale. Watch the fingers of the sun turn red-gold as they stretch to touch the sea.

After lunch, Haim gets up to go and insists on arranging a ride home for me. I shake my head. Mani lingers, pinches my arm so hard I almost cry out. I should leave with Mani. Everything tells me to go with him, *now*. Lydia and Gaby are engrossed in each other. His back to me for the past half-hour. Mohammed hangs around our table, giving Gaby long wistful looks. Scrubbing his area of the table over and over so he can bend over him. Mani leaves, pinching my arm even harder. I wince in pain, tears burn my eyes.

A FISHERMAN LEANING AGAINST THE WALL sings Arab blues. The bright dark colors soften. I can't tell if it's twilight, or still afternoon. Sun's fingers sweep into the sea, find the heart and shatter waves. Foam cracks in the sky. I don't know how long I've been sitting here, lining up their bottles of ale, one by one, on the small table. Gaby orders more ale by holding up two fingers. Mohammed scurries over, makes a production of handing him the bottles, wants the hand contact, refuses to leave until he gets it. I admire him for that. And Lydia.

A while ago Gaby took off his cap and pushed his hair behind his ears, exposing the back of his right ear, the line of his neck. I wait for him to move an inch to the left, or to turn towards the sea, so I can see the way the sideburn grows in, the shadows and muscles of his harsh-stubbled olive cheek, dusted with spicy musk aftershave. When we meet in the heart of the family, he bends his face to me and solemnly turns from left to right so I can kiss his cheeks–thin, stretched taut over high bone. I can just glimpse one of the two deep lines that bracket his mouth. I've become obsessed with these lines. When he talks, they are never still. When he is exasperated, he gnaws the left one. When he laughs, they become dimples. Two lines, indentations of the flesh, carved by an invisible hand, symbolic of his remoteness.

Soon he will stand and lead Lydia to his car and close the door behind them. Drive her somewhere–the beach? Her apartment? He will touch her large high breasts with the long olive fingers that seem eternally curved around an imaginary woman. She will travel up his legs with a shock of discovery. But I sit behind him, unwanted and forgotten, refusing to admit that he will always be the man in the next room. The one I can't have.

I listen to the hoarse murmuring voice. My ear almost touches his shoulder as I strain to hear. "I like to enter a city and see her face. In Lisbon, as soon as I arrive and check in at the hotel, I go out and take a ferry away so I can return from the water. Then Lisbon is beautiful and grand, and I know I'm seeing her face." He pauses, listening to her, then says, "Madrid? Hard to tell. Moorish profiles, Jewish undertones–"

She whispers, and he tilts his head slightly to the left. "That's because you have to come in by water," he says. "I'll bring you in by boat. When you see El Kajda's face, she'll make sense to you." His voice lowers. I can't make out the words anymore. I sit back and play with the bottles of beer, two rows of soldiers on the small, round table.

Mohammed has stopped coming to our table. The café is nearly empty. Only I remain, glued to my chair, facing the impenetrable wall of Gaby's back.

"Little cat." His chair screeches across the floor as he turns to look at me. Silky voice, but freezing eyes. "You've been so quiet. Not joining us. You need another drink."

"I'm going home." I move my chair back. It screeches the way his did, fingernails against a blackboard.

"Not yet. Have some more beer. We'll drink to Sheba." He throws his head back and drinks from the bottle. Looking directly into my eyes, he fumbles for my glass on the table and starts pouring.

It takes me a second to realize what he's doing. By then it's too late. He's pouring beer over my hand, down my arm.

35

It plops to my skirt, down to my ugly bare toes. Lydia leans over his shoulder and gives a sharp, shrill laugh.

Faintly smiling, glassy-eyed, he pours until I jerk to my feet. My elbow shoots out and knocks over the table. We both try to save it, but the bottles topple in all directions. Roll toward the entrance. Shatter at our feet. The smell of warm beer clouds the air.

I feel sick, as if I'm going to vomit. Mohammed shoots me a filthy look as he starts mopping up the mess. I can't face any of them. I start walking out, my sandals crunching on shards of bottles, smashing sardine skeletons.

"Brit! Come back here! You're not mad, are you?"

I turn and see him, arms folded across his chest, as if warding off all of us: me, Lydia, and Mohammed. "I'll take you home. You can't go back alone at night."

"I brought her," says Lydia. "I'll drive her home."

"Give me your address," he tells her. "I'll meet you there as soon as I drop her off."

"I'm not your responsibility. Just drop me off at the Majestic. Mani's probably waiting for me there."

"And the famous Luc. Do whatever you like, but I think you'll want to change first. We both stink of beer."

I give him a dirty look, and he flinches–just barely–but I see it. You knew! I want to shout. Don't pretend you're drunk. You knew exactly what you were doing. But, why?

I don't get any of it.

TOO DEPRESSED TO GO DANCING, I turn off the light in my mother's room and put on my oldest pajamas (red and blue birds dancing across a white sea). I tack my black shawl to the open window to give me some privacy. Through the holes in the shawl, I glimpse bits of sky. When I lick my hand, it tastes like tears.

The hum murmurs through the shawl, tightens around me. It comes and goes, like a revelation. Two things I know: no one hears it but me, and it's meant to lead me somewhere beyond the mellah. When I hear it, I have an immediate urge–almost a *need*–to slip out of my grandparents' house and run down the rue du Soleil through the gate onto the rue Moulay-Youssef, with its shadowy booths lined along the steep hill. And then what? Turn right and descend the hill to the medina and the Place de France? Climb left to the pôterie past the Jardins Publiques to the Ville Nouvelle? Everywhere is forbidden, especially at night, especially for a Jewish girl in an Arab town–born here or not. Danger hisses through the window.

When I peer into the courtyard, I see no one. Not even a cricket, bird, insect. No sign of anything. Only the slouching cats' shadows by the slender palm tree near the kitchen.

Lying back on my mother's narrow bed–under her blue and red velvet tapestry of a prince kidnapping his princess on horseback–I breathe the mimosa she breathed, look at the shadows on the wall that she saw, and wonder if she followed me here, if she is the hum. I close my eyes and find myself wandering in Horsens again, on the other side of the world. I see Dad sitting in the armchair that faces the window of our first floor apartment as he spins the globe of the world. I remember how fast the black seas and gold lands spun around. So fast that I hoped we dizzied Mrs. Kopf, that nosy djinn peering through her curtain across the street. So fast I had to struggle to keep up with Dad. So fast he left my mother far behind, in the bedroom, poring over the photos she'd brought with her from Morocco. The globe whirled, and he laughed. *Pick a place,* he said. *Any place. Pick a name. A religion. A nationality. You can be anyone. Born anywhere.*

Breathless, I watched the spinning globe. Reached out with my finger. To stop the globe. To stop the world. So I could be born. The whirling globe slowed.

Dad looked at my pointing index finger. Scrutinized the black and gold. A mad dictator surveying his provinces. *France,* he said. *No more Jews from Morocco. From now on, we're Christians from Paris. A good choice.*

I see myself telling Gaby—that day in Horsens when time stopped: "I'm a Christian from Paris." The absurdity and stupidity struck me at once but I was too proud to retract my words.

He was quiet while we walked down Candlestick Lane— transformed by his presence into a world in which danger and romance lurked behind each red-brick façade. Moon and sun battled for supremacy in the sky, and Morocco threatened to burst free from its prison beneath the cracks in the sidewalk. We sat on the curb outside Pop Freihofer's store in twilight, sharing penny candies he'd taken at least twenty minutes to choose–debating over the merits of red versus black licorice, and tiny wax bottles of root beer. I even let him have three of the four orange marshmallow circus peanuts we'd gotten.

"It's a good thing you're not a Jew from Morocco," he said, tearing the last stick of strawberry licorice in two and giving me half. "I could tell you stories about this wicked little girl who was born in the house where I grew up. Sultana l'Haoud, the midwife, delivered her. They called her Sultana the Horse because she had six toes on each foot, and she shook the ground when she walked. That little girl was so naughty she wouldn't leave me alone for a minute. She followed me everywhere. I used to carry her in my pocket–like this. But she scratched me. You wouldn't know anything about that, a nice American girl like you. You probably never heard of Aziza, La Beauté de Fez, the naughty girl's great-aunt. Or Kiko–her second cousin. His hair turned white when he was locked overnight in a sla. Oh I forgot, you wouldn't know what a sla is. A place where Jews pray. The rabbi unlocked the door in the morning and found Kiko, his hair the color of snow, and his hands moving like wings."

I stir in my mother's bed and go back farther. When did the hunger begin? The first moment I can pinpoint. Morocco, that dim memory, had already retreated, crouching in the corners of my room in Pennsylvania. I woke up one night, screaming from a nightmare–as usual. But Mom didn't come to sing me "Le rêve bleu." Our apartment was silent. I curled my toes under and hugged myself. The

39

Pretzel Factory's red and blue neon light: 17 REASONS WHY blinked through my open window. Then I saw the cloud wafting toward me. The orange came first, followed by the vanilla. Tart and sweet, like a big gulp of hot mint tea. A Moroccan smell, it made me feel warm and cocooned—as if my mother held me.

The cloud came back at odd moments. When I kissed my best friend, Ti, in the art studio where we took lessons after school, both of us dizzy, pretending we were Heidi and Peter on the Alps. As I approached her, I brushed my lips against hers and almost sank to the floor. An orange-vanilla cloud gathered around me, lifted me, and let me kiss her again and again until we both drew back, our mouths burning, eyes wide in amazement.

The first spring flower I leaned over to pluck on my way to school. I brought it to my nose, breathed deeply, and there it was again: oranges and vanilla circling me, making me weak with hunger.

After night dreams, terrifying in their intensity, the cloud waited to carry me back to safety, my room on the corner of Candlestick and Wise.

I asked my mother about the fragrant cloud. She puzzled over it awhile, then one day when I came home from school to find her perched on her little stepladder, layering wallpaper, she turned and said, "The potters' soap. My brother, Gaby. He was an apprentice at the Arab pôterie, and he used to come home with his hands smelling of oranges and vanilla. The soap the potters used."

"Gaby?" I asked, enjoying the sound of his name. Gah-bee.

"The one and only." She studied the latest wallpaper: lime-green watering cans sprinkling endless showers of water over pale yellow blossoms. "The black sheep of the family. My baby brother. I remember when he was born. I was seven, and Maman set him in the center of their big bed. He was so sweet, with a head full of black curls, and a red face, lying in the center of the bed like a tiny king. Like Moses floating in the sea. You couldn't see how handsome he was going to be yet. Or what a rascal. He used to run away from home at least once a week. And count on me to bring him food. Always in trouble."

"But why would I smell potters' soap?"

"You were crazy about him. Trailed after him, even up to Papa's roof terrace. Only Gaby and Elie were allowed to go there, but you tagged along until Papa let you in, too. Gaby called you his little cat because you clawed at anyone who tried to get near him."

"I don't believe that! It doesn't sound anything like me!"

She sighed and climbed down from the ladder. "You're just like your father. And like Gaby too. A rebel against nature. Come with me."

I followed her to the room she and Dad shared. Large bed, sheepskin rug on the floor, the shoebox of photos. I stretched on the sheepskin, imagining myself as Cigarette, the dancing girl in Ouida's book about the French Foreign Legion. I spied in the Sahara for the British soldier I loved.

41

"Here," Mom said, handing me a photograph, about four by six inches. "This was taken right before we left El Kajda. You're six, and he must be about seventeen."

I hesitated before looking at it. Too much to absorb—too many layers, too many things all happening at once. The tough nubby coils of the sheepskin against my bare legs. Dots of paste on Mom's slender fingers as she handed me the photo. Blue shafts of light shot through the room.

The photo was on heavy beige paper, edges cracked and broken. On the back, someone had written in quavering blue ink: "Gabriel Afriat and Brites Suleika Lek, 1957." I turned it over and saw a black and white photo of a little girl sitting on a young man's lap. His chin rested on her head. Their dark curls mingled together. An embroidered band was tied around her forehead. When I try to remember why the photo shocked me so much, I have to dissect it in order to be true and precise. It wasn't his beauty that startled me, dazzling as it was, even in a brittle, yellowing photo: a sharp-boned face with light, almond-slanted eyes, a straight nose I'd have given anything for, and full lips. Unsmiling, as fierce as the tiny warrior who gripped his hands across her flat chest. It wasn't even the exotic embroidered band across my forehead—although that did give me a momentary start: the foreignness of this creature who was me, had to be me, but in some fundamental, impossible way, was not me. It wasn't the way I held onto him for dear life, daring the photographer—or anyone—to pry me from him. Although that too frightened me later—in the dark—when I tried to recall what it must have felt like to want someone that badly, to cling to another person so openly. To be so naked.

This photo was proof that I'd lived before Horsens, hadn't just sprouted on this snowy ground–a Christian from Paris–with no past, no family apart from my parents, no memories. I had existed in another world before this one. A Gaby-and-Brit world, one in which I had loved, and obviously had known great pain and joy. None of which I remembered.

Who was I then, this bland one-dimensional American Brit? I touched little foreign Brit, her frowning mouth–upper lip over thinner lower lip, enormous dark eyes, stubby nose, chubby legs dangling over his.

That night I put the photo of Gaby and Brit under my pillow and lay on my bed, eyes open. As if I were dreaming (and yet I knew I was wide awake, staring at the neon 17 REASONS WHY), birds flew in the open window (which I knew was closed) and surrounded me in a mad flutter of wings. I was in both places at once. My grandfather handed us brushes and buckets of red, green, and blue paint, and Gaby and I painted their wings. The wind blew at us, almost blew us off the roof, but we struggled until the birds were streaked with color. *Write your wish*, Papa Naphtali said. I watched Gaby scribble on a scrap of paper and wrap it around a red-painted pigeon's leg. He let the bird go and turned to me, his face blocking the sun. *Hurry, little cat!* I already wanted so much there was no way I could squeeze it onto a small piece of paper. And I didn't yet know how to write many words. But as he leaned closer, his dark restless face lit with mischief, I knew that there was only one word I could write, the only one that captured all my hunger for the world and life and mystery.

I HEAR FOOTSTEPS ON THE MARBLE TILES of the courtyard and the sound of a match being struck. I peer through the holes of my shawl. He's out there, leaning against the mimosa tree, smoking. This is my chance. I leave my room, tiptoe down the hall, and see the blue door, ajar.

*And in the spring of 1865* it came to pass that Alfred Dehodencq, a French artist living in Tangiers, painted Suleika's execution. He spent months working on the huge canvas. His painting depicts the moment of her death. The crowds gathered in the square to watch. Eyes—bloodthirsty, weeping, horrified—dominate the canvas.

Suleika's story fastened onto Dehodencq's soul the way it did to so many others. He spoke to people who had known her family. As he inquired into her death, a different story began to emerge, one involving an Arab lover, implying that perhaps saintly Suleika was not so saintly after all. She fell in love, converted to Islam, then tried to return to Judaism. The Arabs refused to let her go: You recited the Shahada, the Formula of Conversion. Now you belong to us. They ordered her beheaded as a lapsed convert.

During the months he works on Suleika's painting, Dehodencq sees her everywhere he looks, even as he sips Pernod in his favorite café at the entrance to the Great Socco. Her face is always cloaked by her hair. Her beauty tantalizes, leads him down streets he cannot remember walking, through doorways he cannot remember entering. He must see her eyes in order to finish the painting. Only one glimpse.

Does she turn and look at him directly?

One night, after wandering through Tangiers in feverish pursuit of Suleika, he returns to his studio and paints until he can paint no more. He stares at the canvas—blood racing, head pounding—and knows he has just completed his masterwork, the one that will make his reputation in Paris. He will return to France and exhibit the painting in galleries.

He tries to sleep, but his mind is restless. He gets up and goes out again, down the familiar streets of Tangiers, and makes his way to the sea. He stands at the edge of the sea, marking the border of Africa, where the wind blows ferociously, and stares at the Rock of Gibraltar. He has been in this land too long.

*The wind, sun, voices, doors have put a spell on him. For him, Morocco is em-bodied in the name of an elusive girl whom he has touched only in his dreams at night, or when he brushes her face and body with a lover's delicate strokes.*

*He inhales the fresh salt air and slowly feels his mind clearing. Suleika is dead, but he is alive. It is time to leave behind this obsession. He walks home. The door is blown open, the painting slashed—the canvas hanging in tatters, destroyed beyond any possibility of repair.*

*That very day, Dehodencq leaves Tangiers. He is forgotten, except in the memories of certain Tangerinos who recall the artist in his wide black hat and cape, hurrying down one street after another, gesturing and crying out to someone who is always a few steps beyond.*

—Rafael Pinto,
*Recuerdos de un viejo tangerino, 1879*

# *homing pigeon*

THEY WARN ME ABOUT SHEBA'S GIRL—as if I'm
going to lunge on my niece, chew her up and
spit her out in pieces. I'm sick to death of it. As if
they think I have no control. As if I don't see my
sister in her eyes and startled laugh. As if—

But no one knows me. No one understands. Only my father senses it sometimes, the great joke that was played on
me, the gap between what I look like, and what I am. And
even he warned me today: *you lay a hand on Sheba's girl
and I'll kill you.*

They think she's in love with me. They don't see how lost
she is. A little cat searching for her mother in me. It would
take much more than an American schoolgirl to make me
lose control. Only once, two years ago, did I lose it. And even
then, when I look back, I walked into the trap, eyes open.
The fool that I was, seeing what existed only in my need.

SHE WANTED ME ROUGH. It's in every creature to be violent,
but I recoil from it. Always. I am gentle with the clay when I
curve my fingers around it. You don't hear a song by trampling it beneath your feet. My brother-in-law Haim claims a

47

woman needs brutality from a man. To be tamed and beaten and kept in her place. But look at my sister Mamouche: a wounded, fluttering bird. Demure and silenced, the way she never was when we were growing up.

I wanted to hear Estrella's song, tried to listen with my fingers touching her body. She screamed and cursed me in Arabic. I moved back and looked at her. My bride. Bloodshot black eyes. Mouth spitting curses. She screamed, cried, worked herself into a rage. I watched in horrified curiosity. Not sure how to approach, or even if I should approach.

My silence, my waiting made her crazier.

I wasn't scared. Not yet. Still wondering. Waiting.

She didn't quiet. She didn't calm. She started kicking me, pounding my chest with her fists, screeching curses.

I bent over her–like a turtle's shell–and held her wrists down on the bed. I started telling her a story. One of my father's. About a prince and the gold bird he loves. I talked without thinking. Only to silence the screams and stop the kicking. I spoke in a whisper to force her to listen. My hands were gentle restraints. If she wanted to pounce on me again, she could–easily.

I was still trying to understand. My voice as tentative as my hands. By the time I finished my story, she was lying still. Tear-stained, splotchy red face staring up at me.

"Estrella," I said. "Did you like the story?"

She jerked her chin up and down.

"Did you hear how the bird came to sing for the prince? When he set her free, she returned to him of her own will and sang for him. And turned into a beautiful princess. And they lived happily ever after in their garden."

She jerked her chin again.

I kissed her mouth. She bit me. I bit her back—lightly. She bit my tongue so hard I had to pry her teeth apart to free myself. I sat up, swallowing blood.

She shivered and rolled over on the bed, showing me her seashell cheeks. The bed quivered with her. "Beat me!" she said over her shoulder. "I've been bad! You must beat me!"

I SPENT MY WEDDING NIGHT MOVING between the front steps and the bedroom. Out for a cigarette to stare at the moon. "Moses' face," my mother used to say, "Never look at him directly. If you see his face, he'll put a spell on you."

"But isn't he a good guy?" I'd ask. "Why would he put a spell on me?"

"Oh, Gaby," she'd say with a sigh. "Too many questions."

Caught. At twenty-seven. By what? A vision that appeared in our house one evening after dinner. A friend of a cousin of Tonton Menasseh, visiting from Tetouan. A strange, ugly, pockmarked man who brought his sister and her daughter to visit. His face was scarred and punctured, a red-purple mask of self-inflicted wounds. But his niece was an unusual beauty: about twenty-one, with uncombed wild black hair, jittery moves that made me want to soothe her the way I do my cats, and mad, restless eyes that reminded me of Tuhami's mad, restless hands. What I didn't know yet was that she destroyed, and he created. In the end, what's the difference? To create, or to destroy? With clay, you create over the destroyed piece. Nothing is ever thrown away or lost. Even the pieces that crack in the sun, or that lose their center. The memory lingers in your fingertips.

"Listen to the clay," Tuhami used to say, holding up his hands and pressing them against my ears.

I let her see me. Vain bastard, Perla would say. Vain? No. Pragmatic. I use what I have to get what I need. In spite of her wildness, she was an innocent. She stared at me, mouth gaping. Your face has been marked by God, my mother had told me. For better or worse.

I smiled. She stared until her mother pulled her away.

I left the room and went into the courtyard. The pock-marked uncle followed me. For a dance party, Mani had hung orange paper lanterns on the mimosa tree. The long heavy branches barely swung in the night breeze. I was excited, the way I hadn't been over a woman since I'd returned from the ship. Awake, the way I feel when I look up from the clay and realize that seven or eight hours have passed. I forget food. I am blue with cold. Tuhami and the other potters are gone. Shivering, lips trembling, I cover the piece, wash up and go back outside. Light a cigarette and watch the sky. Tuhami hates the return to the world. I love it. The sky burns red. A black stork lands on one of the jars drying on the terrace. I let the air enter me. It whistles through me the way the wind did on the ship: I *was* the wind.

The uncle and I smoked while he told me about her. She's beautiful, the youngest in a fine family from Tetouan, has a lovely singing voice, is sweet and docile, the ideal woman . . .

He was reeling me in, but I let the words wash over me. I'd heard them too many times before–from brothers, fathers, uncles, once even a dying husband who wanted me to take his wife after he was gone. I'd grown skilled at listening without hearing, at not saying a word that would commit me. Sometimes for the thrill of the game, I let myself be caught–but always with a way out. I had just broken off an engagement to Maya by letting her see me at the Majestic with Joëlle. There was always a loophole, a way to escape the net. What I'd never counted on was that I'd walk into the trap, eyes open. His banal sales pitch went unheard. I was caught from the moment I heard her laugh.

She came into the courtyard with her mother and stood at Sheba's window. After a moment she started laughing. The lantern light didn't reach her face. I glimpsed shadows and gleaming teeth. Her laugh rippled through me like the sea. Curled over the edge, slapped against my chest like a tidal wave. For a second I smelled salt and saw the sunset glow in Moses' eyes.

The uncle nudged me. "Hey Don Juan, we've heard all about you in Tetouan. But this one comes with a price. A ketubah. You want to fuck her, you have to marry her."

I ignored him. The siren-laugh drew me. Wild and uncontrolled as her beauty, it promised freedom. I smiled in the dark and advanced.

I've replayed this scene endlessly in my mind. His words,

her laugh, my steps toward her. As if there's a clue to be found. A truth that's escaped me. A gap through which I could have slipped. But I missed all clues, truths, loopholes. I walked toward her the way I walked toward Tuhami the first time I saw him.

I had ducked into the pôterie, running like mad from the Arab kids who were pelting us with stones. Samy Sasportas and Georges Attias stayed to fight. I ran. (*Gaby's problem*, wrote my teacher in a note to my parents, *is that even if a bully picks on him, he doesn't fight back. He runs to the class-room. When asked why, he said, "I don't like to fight."*)

I went past the tents and booths where the potters sold their pieces, to the hill where they worked, dotted with large beehive kilns and sloped terraces stacked with cups, bowls, and dishes drying in the air. A line of potters sat at their wheels under blinding sun. Unhesitatingly I went to Tuhami and stood before him. Nut-brown little man, eyes closed, he hugged the clay the way I hugged Lise, my girlfriend. He ap-peared porous, open as the sun and sky, the clay itself. The wheel spun. He smiled, tilted his head to one side. The mound grew. He sliced. A kid gave him another mound of clay. He flexed his hands, touched the clay, kicked the stand, and the wheel spun again.

I came every day after school to watch. He never spoke to me, I didn't speak to him. I was a Jewish kid on a hill of Arab potters—enough that he let me watch without chasing me away.

He told me later, "You mimicked my moves with your hands. I knew even then you had the power in you."

"Why didn't you talk to me?" I asked him.

He shook his head.

I didn't push. Tuhami has the best sense of timing of any man I know. The precise instant when to stop the wheel. When to stop working on a piece.

I sat fumbling over a bowl that refused to sit straight, its center somewhere on the side. I fought with it. The more I fought, the uglier and more lopsided it became. He told me: "Ten minutes, my boy. No longer. If you don't find the center in ten minutes, move to the next piece."

After I began working as his apprentice and the girls started tracking me to the pôterie, he told me: "I've been watching you. You do the same thing with girls. Ten minutes, and on to the next."

But it's not true. I didn't want them. I wasn't searching for their center. They didn't make me feel less alone. They didn't hear me the way the clay did. Sometimes I talked to them with my hands. Sometimes it helped for a while.

I watch couples to see what they talk about. What they find ceaselessly fascinating about each other. Even eavesdropping, I feel faint from boredom. The waste. All these bodies and minds dedicated to—what? Killing time? It's all so small. We're so small.

On the sea I understood, the way I do with the clay. I won't argue with my father about God. I'm not a debater. I can't keep a discussion spinning in the air. I get so intrigued by what the other person says, what's behind his eyes or voice, or the way he jabs the air with his index finger to make a point, that often I find myself swaying to his side.

But not about this. There are things I *know*. Beyond words. Even beyond touch. I know that in our terror we created gods that care, angels that watch over us, demons that punish. I don't believe in the gods but I believe in the stories. Maybe because I heard my father's tales on his terrace, wind blowing our hair back, sun dancing across our faces and hands. We were like birds, crouched on the white chalk roof, ready to fly.

When I watched Tuhami, I heard him sing softly, beneath the rumble of the wheel, the voices of the other potters, the kilns hissing as they fired, the tourists shrieking for bargains behind me. He sang to himself and smiled as he worked. One day he got up, threw a slab of clay on the wheel, and said, "Make something!"

The terror I felt is the same I felt on my wedding night, staring at my wife's face in sleep. Still breathing in ragged bursts, one fist clenched at her chin. I'd refused to beat her. She brought me my belt. Bent over my knees. I pushed her from me. She took one of my small clay jars and threw it at me. I didn't move. It thudded against my chest, fell to the floor, and shattered. I walked back and forth, barefoot, on clay shards all night.

"Punish me!" she screamed. "Punish me! Show me you love me! Prove you're a man!"

Earlier that night I had talked to her, fed her, made her tea with sheba. I drew her onto my lap and rocked her, tried to get to the heart, to understand. She calmed for a few minutes, then started screaming, cursing, kicking again. She didn't want me to touch her, hold her, do anything but beat her. She put the belt in my hand. I felt the sharp buckle dig into my palm and looked at her. Eyes crossed. Darting to all sides at once. Tongue hanging out. Panting, like a sick puppy I'd brought home once. "Beat me! I'm so bad!"

I shut my eyes. Tried to hear the wind through the waves, the song of the clay. She screamed at me again. Threw the cup of hot tea on me. Began shouting for her mother, for God to take her from this weakling she'd married, this poor excuse of a man. She cursed me with words fouler than the fishermen at the port used, fouler than any sailor.

I blocked my ears, listened harder for the wind.


IN THE MORNING HAIM, Simon, my uncle Menasseh, and Mani came to wish us well. They found me outside, in a teeshirt and my torn fishing pants. Unshaven, red-eyed, smoking.

"Well, you haven't slept a wink," said Haim. "That's as it should be."

"Ah, newlyweds," said Simon. "I remember when Perla and I couldn't keep our hands off each other."

"Show her who's boss from the beginning," said Haim. "Otherwise she'll take over. A woman needs to know her place. Only then is she content."

Mani watched me without saying a word. His wig flopping over one eye like a black-eyed duck I saw once. He blinked and blinked.

The others laughed and waited for me to say something.

ONE NIGHT I DIDN'T RETURN HOME AFTER WORK. I saw her coming from the cottage toward the factory. The cottage was a mistake. I bought it with the money I'd saved from the ship. The money that I was going to smuggle out of the country to get my parents and me to Israel. I'd blown all my savings, and now, we were isolated, and I was broke. Nowhere to go, and nothing to look forward to. Meanwhile Haim resents me more than ever. No other young couples can afford to live alone. Especially not in a little yellow house that should be in the woods of my father's tales, but instead sits smack in factory fumes and smells of the port. It's not enough that I smell the sardines all day at work. They're at home too. In the sheets, behind her ears, caught in my throat. I am turning into a fish, unable to breathe air or water.

Every day after work, she comes closer. Soon she'll be on the other side of the factory door, waiting for me. It won't take long before she opens the clanging doors to track me down. She sniffs me out. I hide in the bathroom, head in my hands, while she goes through the house looking for me. If she doesn't find me, she instantly panics. No middle ground. No transitions between moods. I thought I came from a crazy family. All of us shouting, arguing, my father retreating to the roof, my mother coming into our rooms at night to put spells on us. I lived in a world of women–my mother, Sheba, Perla and Mamouche–all plotting, whispering, laughing, crying. My father pulled me upstairs to his world. The roof belonged to the women too, but he took it over. I helped him build the terrace, the tented area he wanted to protect his divan, books, and oud. An archway divided the covered world from the roofless one. He bought two enormous brass cages and filled them with fifty pigeons. He wouldn't let me give them names or make them my pets. I was always bringing home stray cats and fallen birds. "The pigeons are free," he told me. "Here is the secret to training a wild animal, the key to understanding freedom. Never lock the cage. Never close the gate."

He opened the cages, and the pigeons flew away, the sky filled with whirring, wings flapping, piercing cries. When they were gone, the sky the same windy gray it usually was, he told me the story of the prince and the gold bird. Before he even finished the tale, the birds began returning, entering the open cages, pecking at our hands and feet.

"Gaby, are you in there?" She knocks on the bathroom door. Within thirty seconds, her voice will rise to a hysterical shriek. She'll scream and cry, and when I come out, I'll find her flailing at the floor, or beating her head against the wall.

Her yellow dress whipping around her legs, hand shadowing her eyes, she searched for me in the stream of workers leaving the factory. Haim nudged me. "You lucky bastard, she can't wait, eh? That's how a wife should be."

I looked at Haim's envious little eyes. He won't help. As he went down the factory steps, I gripped Simon and held him back. "Tell her I had to stay late. I'm—I need something in town. I'll go the back way."

"Is everything okay? If you had a fight, the best thing is to talk it out."

"Simon."

He must have seen the desperation in my eyes because he nodded. I took off in a flash, winding my way around the line of factories, through the sandy, grassy fields. I didn't know where I was going. At first I thought: to dive from the Djorf Yihoudi—rising high, rocky: a cliff where Jews die. But I found myself running to the pôterie. I hadn't been there once in the three months we'd been married. The scenes weren't worth it. *Why do you want to abandon me? To play in dirt and mud with Arabs? Why? And why do you want to see your father? Why can't I go on his roof with you? Why must I wait outside the door? Why do you want to leave me alone, worrying about you? Tell your father to come here.*

Even the roof had become tainted. I felt her breathing behind the stained-glass door, waiting.

"Gaby? Let me in. Should I run a bath for you? Wash your feet?"

I sat in the bathroom and smelled my sardine fingers. And behind the sardines, the jasmine woman from Kobe who laughed at jokes I never understood. And behind the jasmine, the wine-sweet nipples of the gypsy in Portugal who swore she'd seen my face in a dream before she met me

and whose father and brothers chased me back to the ship.
And always, under everything, the potter's soap—oranges
and vanilla. It hadn't always been like this. I'd had a life before I married her.

She pounded on the door until I let her in. The crossed
eyes I couldn't look at anymore. The smile that never fit her
face, the occasion, anything. The smell of her: dead, rotting.
Sardines left too long in the warehouse. I shut my eyes and
she washed my feet and kissed them. And that night in bed
insisted that I must beat her the way a man does, for all the
bad things she'd done.

When I arrived at the pôterie, I was shaking so hard it
was difficult to slow down, to form words. Tuhami saw me
and wouldn't let me sit at the wheel. "Not yet," he said. "Tea
first." We sat in his tent behind the line of potter's wheels. I
heard the tourists shouting for bargains and the potters arguing back. I smelled clay and dust and raw earth. We dug
up our own clay farther up on the hill. This was my dirt, my
land, my smells.

"Drink your tea, my son," he said, watching me. He
wanted to know what was wrong, why I hadn't come in
months, why I shivered as if a djinn shook my ribs from inside. But he wouldn't say a word. He waited, and after a
while, I felt calm again. My hands itching to dig into the clay,
to work. To forget. To remember what came before.

I went to Tuhami's wheel. Even after all these years, I
didn't have one of my own. Too many of the men resented
me, the only Jew on a hill of Arabs. Without Tuhami, I don't

believe they'd have let me work. My second father. And the clay, my love. The only love.

"Work the clay first. Wedge it good and hard," he told me and let me go.

I pounded and wedged and kneaded the clay as if it were my own cursed life. I beat it the way she insisted I beat her. *If you were a man, you'd hit me until I turned black and blue!* she'd cry. I didn't want to hate her. I didn't want to hate her mother for pretending her daughter was a good little girl, too sheltered to meet with me alone before marriage, unprotected by a father—Perla told me he'd run off with another woman. Her hollowed, punctured uncle.

Little things. Inexplicable things. She never flushes the toilet. She tries on my clothes when I'm at work and leaves them wrinkled, crumpled on the bed. She puts on makeup with a heavy, unsteady hand. Her clothes never fit. I have to check her before we go out: skirt on backwards, ears filthy, hair uncombed, lipstick mustache, sour breath because she forgot to brush her teeth. She doesn't wash unless I tell her to. I realize now that her mother must have taken care of her until she handed her over to me. But how could she leave her daughter with a stranger? Knowing how helpless she is? How could she return to Tetouan and not once try to contact us and ask how she is? That stuns me more than anything else. As if the moment Estrella were gone, she ceased to exist for them. Exactly what frightens Estrella about me: every time I walk out the door without her, it's as if I no longer exist. Or as if she doesn't.

I sat at the wheel, hunched my shoulders, kicked the foot lever, and hugged the clay that I'd pounded into submission. Hugged her, oh God, with my hands, my soul, my heart. Pressed her between my thighs. Fucked her steadily until the sun set, and at last, she cried out.

I slept in the underground shed. Didn't go to work the next morning. Knew she'd panic but I couldn't go back. Couldn't look at those eyes and smell that dead wet smell, listen to the voice rising in hysteria.

You think this is how a woman should be, Haim, you asshole? This is what you want, you fuckhead?

"Gaby, let me sit on your lap while you eat. Let me feed you."

"I don't need to be fed. Why don't you just sit down and eat? We'll eat side by side."

"I'll eat after you, the way a woman should. A woman should never eat at the same time as her husband. I'll eat your crumbs."

Or picture the happy couple in their living room. She sits on the arm of my chair as I try to turn the pages of the newspaper.

"What's that you're reading?"

*"Le petit marocain."*

"What does it say?"

"The news. Here. Take a section. Read for yourself."

"I want you to read it to me. That way we get the same news."

Breathing over my shoulder, in my ear. I put down the

newspaper. "Let's have some music. What do you like, chérie?"

"What do *you* like?"

"I like all kinds of music. I'm asking what *you* like to hear."

"I like all kinds."

"But what kind in particular?"

"All kinds. I'll put it on. Whatever you like to hear."

"On second thought I don't really want to hear anything. I don't really like music."

"I don't really like it either. Wait! Where are you going?"

"Out for a cigarette."

"Out? Why? Smoke here! I'll hold the ashtray for you. Why do you need to go out?"

The potters are coming in. Early morning. Time for them to begin their day. What would I give to stay here, underground in this shed for the rest of my life, and forget everything else? Most of them greet me, but a few give me wary looks. Tuhami's crazy Jew. They can stay here and dig into the clay, work it and carve it until their shoulders are aching. While I have to go to the fiery pit, sardines and women's heads and hands moving like robots. And her, crossed eyes, throwing herself at my feet. "I've been bad. So bad. Punish me!"

I remember my dream. Somewhere in the desert, sand blowing in my eyes. I taste sand, grit, dust. The sand is not the heavy gold sand of El Kajda, but pale, soft, burning hot. Sahara sand, blowing, blowing. In the storm I see a light. I follow it on my hands and knees. It comes from inside a cave.

I start working and shut my eyes so my fingers can remember more clearly. It has to be huge. Vast. A vessel from Ali Baba's cave transplanted to the city. The desert. A fist punching the sky, tearing through the veil. I inch my way step by step. Patient. Seeing what is coming: the light I have to create inside. With no idea how I'm going to get there. Only that I must get there. The light draws me. I talk to no one. I can't lose the vision. Tuhami brings me bread, a slab of hard cheese, a bottle of mineral water, an orange. The orange inspires me, adds to the vision. She's the light, round and eternal: a moon. A moon inside. Reflected light. The lantern and mimosa. Her laugh. A woman in the desert. Hiding. The orange protecting her secret. Who hurt you? Why do you need to be punished? What do you see behind crossed eyes?

My body forces me to stop. I need to piss, eat, drink, have a cigarette. I need air. I spray my vessel with water, cover her with damp plastic wrap, wash my hands, grab the food and water, the orange, and climb the steps.

It's sunset. I used to love dawn most. The promise of something more. The surprise of another day. I imagined myself living in early days when no one knew for sure that day followed night, that the dark didn't simply mean the end. Every new morning was a gift. I'd ride my bike to the Djorf Yihoudi and dive into the freezing Atlantic and swim as far from Morocco as I could. I tried to reach the black line. I didn't think of it as the horizon, but as the line separating me from a new world. When I reached the black line, I knew everything would change. We would all be free. Cage doors opened. My father back down on earth. I swam and swam until one day I touched the black line. I almost cried in joy. I looked up and saw I'd reached a ship. Sailors grinned down at me. They let me on the ship, gave me bitter coffee and sesame biscuits. Then I swam back. I'd found the gateway, the hole in the wall.

On the ship I learned to love sunset. The sun, fiery and intense, burning the water. A moment when the whole world was on fire: sky, sun, sea, rising moon, our own faces. The moment I live for. Sailors recognize each other on land. The sunset still glows in our eyes.

Only Ibrahim, the night watchman, remains on the hill, guarding the armies of cups, bowls, urns, jars, and pitchers, drying on sloped terraces. On his tiny grill, he broils tomatoes. We eat them and smoke. And then I get up and go home.

She's sitting naked in the tub. My razor in her hand. Cutting slits up her arms and down her thighs. For each hour I was away. Twenty-one. Twenty-two. Twenty-three.

THE LOCUSTS CAME THAT SUMMER. The sky was dark, almost black. Rabbi Eliahu ran through the streets, shrieking, "It's a plague from God! We're sinners! We haven't kept the commandments!"

## homing pigeon

She was terrified of everything: shadows, the dark, sudden sounds, people, animals. My cats were monsters. My sisters, witches putting spells on her. My father, her enemy. The factory, a prison that kept me away from her. I stopped going to the pôterie. She waited for me at the factory door, and we walked to the cottage together in a silence as thick as the blackened sky.

The locusts ate all the grain that summer, all the wheat and corn. The fields were empty. We had no bread, no food. Vendors sold the locusts, fat on the wheat they'd devoured. You'd hear them call, "Locusts! Sweet and rich! Eat them hot!" She couldn't bear to look at them, to touch them. But she kneeled at my legs and cracked them open. Fed me with her hands. I was a man. I had to stay strong.

At night she screamed that I wasn't enough of a man. A real man would whip her day and night, leave her black and blue. She wanted marks, signs on her flesh that I belonged to her and that she belonged to me.

Sex wasn't what she wanted from me. Not touch either. I think she hated being touched. Something had happened to her and was instantly hushed. By the time she came to me, it was already too buried and inert. There was no way for me to reach her.

I know my father beat my mother. I heard her cry in her room. Haim beats Mamouche. I don't think Simon beats Perla: she'd give him a right hook that would knock him flat. And Sheba's eyes would stop a man in his tracks. But most men beat their wives. My first woman–Madame Moyal, my

65

seventh grade teacher–bared her breasts to me after school one day, and then told me to slap her face and breasts lightly, the way her husband did. "Because what we're doing is wicked," she said, "and it will show that you love me."

I tried to get Perla and Mamouche to make friends with Estrella. She didn't want friends. She didn't go out. She talked to no one but me. In public she was completely silent. No one saw the extremes of her behavior. No one could even guess. And I couldn't tell anyone about her. But I wasn't supposed to have friends either, or go out, or talk to anyone but her. If I came home unexpectedly during the day, I found her in bed, eyes open, staring at the wall. It took a while for her eyes to focus and see me again.

I insisted she go to a doctor. He examined her and told me she was a normal woman with typical female complaints. He said, "It's perfectly natural for a woman to want to stay home and see no one but her husband. Give her a baby. That will make her happy and fulfilled. A woman without a baby has too much time to think."

I brought her to my mother, who took one look at her and said, "Give her to me for a month. She needs powerful healing." I knew my mother could take care of her–if anyone could–but Estrella dug her heels in the ground and refused. Absolutely refused. "I'm your wife now. I belong to you. I can't leave you. Ever."

And so we went on, in our idyllic cottage, living our fairy tale lives.

I dreamed of the sea, of the vessel I'd left unfinished in the shed. Tuhami came to see me at the factory. I didn't explain, but he understood. He asked me why I didn't leave her. I'm always the one who leaves. Sometimes I wait too long, until it begins to get messy, but usually I manage to glide from one to another. I can't leave. I can't talk to anyone but my father. And even he doesn't know the full story. It's as if her way of thinking has spread to me, as if I need to be punished too, for my women, for being who I am, what I am. A validation of everyone's ominous predictions: Gaby will come to a bad end. He crosses the border into the Arab world. Gaby will be killed one day by a jealous husband, or an Arab at the port or the pôterie. Mothers warn their daughters: you're better off with an ugly man. A handsome man will play you for a sucker. Just look at Gaby. If they knew about my marriage, I'd be the ironic punch line to every joke. But that's not what stops me. I look into her eyes and see the terror and rage no one else does. But instead of running, I'm paralyzed, the way I am in a nightmare. They left her alone. Can I do the same?

Tuhami told me he knew a place I could hide, with his family in the mountains. A place where I'd be left alone until I decided to return. I made him promise to fire my vessel, to keep her safe for me. She wasn't finished. I held what I still needed to do in my mind. A corner in back, the only place Estrella hadn't invaded.

Even Haim finally saw that something was wrong,

although in his eyes, it made no sense since I had the perfect wife. He let me go on the fishing boats instead of staying in the factory. I spent the day on the ocean with the fishermen. We were so busy I couldn't think. When we returned to the port, I saw the Djorf Yihoudi, and I held that too in my mind: the last hope when everything else was gone.

She fed me, washed me, watched me, breathed on me, echoed my words. Huddled behind the stained glass door of the roof when I talked to my father. "Try again," he told me. "Marriage is a sacred vow. She's mad. You can't divorce a madwoman. Make your life away from her. You don't need advice on that. You've always done what you wanted. Whether it was joining the Arabs at the pôterie, or leaving on the ship, or going with every woman in town."

To create something stronger and more eternal than I am. To be free. All I've ever wanted. Since the day we painted the pigeons and scrolled our secret wishes around their legs– and watched them fly. Little Brit was tagging along with me as usual, so I let her follow me to the roof, and the three of us painted the pigeons' wings with coarse-bristled brushes. Red, green, blue. The bright colors of the bobbing fishing boats. Soon we were surrounded by a mad throbbing of painted wings, beating fast as hummingbirds.

What happened? Where did I go wrong? Should I have stayed on the ship forever, circling the seas?

"I can't breathe," I told my father. "I'm going to die."

A week later Joëlle came to the factory. I ignored her. Everywhere I looked, I saw Estrella's crossed eyes, heard her sudden senseless laugh. Joëlle hung in, came to the port three or four days in a row. Knew I'd eventually meet her eyes, the way I had when I was engaged to Maya.

She waited until I glanced up one day after work, and said, "Mon beau, you know I'm addicted to you. Can't get you out of my system. Look." She held out trembling hands. "I'm suffering withdrawal from you."

I grasped the words, for the first time needing them the way a woman does.

That night, I tried again, as we sat on the sofa. "Talk to me, Estrella. Let's start again. We don't have to be rough, you and I. We can be friends, lovers. It doesn't have to be this way."

Her eyes glazed. She didn't hear me.

"Are you listening? Do you understand me?"

She got up restlessly, went to the bedroom and returned with my black leather belt. "Show me you love me. Make me a good girl. Make me be good. Then I'll listen to everything you say."

She pulled down her pants and bent over my knees, bare ass in the air, and I cracked. Slapped her. She cried out, and I stopped immediately. "Harder! Harder! Use the belt!" I refused. My hand on her ass degrading enough. For a fleeting second, I felt a sort of thrill: her submission, my domination—but after that second, it passed. And I was faced with my hand slapping her pale quivering rump. The stain spreading from my fingers to my hand and wrist, to my soul. My stomach coiled in on itself, tight, a snake. She smelled like garlic and sardines. I couldn't bear the smell. My stained, dark hand beating methodically until it ached. "That's it," I said, thrusting her from me. "It's over."

She curled back on my lap like a child and kissed me on the mouth for the first time.

On the terrace, we wrote our wishes on small pieces of paper. *To be free*, I wrote. I wound the paper tightly around a red pigeon's bamboo-stalk leg and watched him rise in a flurry of wings and rustles. I saw myself gripping his wings and flying behind him, a Jewish Icarus, soaring to places Jews weren't permitted to go.

"True freedom requires a cold heart," my father told me as we watched the painted pigeons fly. "You can't prefer prison." He locked the empty brass cages so they couldn't return, even if they wanted to.

I waded in from the fishing boat the next day, Samir and I pulling in the nets. Joëlle stood at the edge of the water, waiting for me. A copper woman. Gold in the setting sun. Smiling, she held out her hands to me.

I gave the net to Samir and waded the rest of the way to her. Pulled her against my wet body and kissed her. Hard and long. She tasted like the tomatoes Ibrahim and I grilled an eternity ago. She tasted alive.

I don't know how many times we fucked that night. I hadn't realized how starving I was. "You are my bread," I told her. "My water."

She laughed, and I reached for her again. A warm, burnished woman. Dark red hair, red-brown eyes, gold-copper skin. The texture of her flesh dense and rich. Her body solid, her voice real. Eyes that smiled. Everything in that bed made sense. Our hunger, our bodies touching, the smell and taste of her.

At dawn, we sat in bed and talked, drank coffee. She wanted to know about my marriage. She told me that everyone in town was sure I was cheating on Estrella, had been since the beginning. "You're the first," I told her. "And the last. I want out."

"Move in with me," she said. "No obligations. No demands. I love you. I always have. But I won't ask for anything you don't want to give."

I went straight to work at the factory. Hope in my heart for the first time in six months. I had to break free. I couldn't return to that death. Not another day. Not another night. I'd take her back to Tetouan myself, to her family. I had to talk to her, to make her see there was no future for us in this farce of a marriage. I went home during my lunch hour, dreading even entering the yellow cottage. I opened the door. Inside, it smelled musty, already abandoned. Thick-stranded resentment and rage clouding the air. A heavy brooding silence. Too heavy. Too brooding.

A sound suddenly. In the kitchen. I ran and stopped in the doorway. She stood naked by the sink, pouring a can of kerosene over herself.

"Estrella!" I screamed.

She struck a match, and flames engulfed her. In an instant, she seemed to explode.

71

I grabbed my wool sweater hanging on a hook and dove into the flames. Her hair was on fire. Already I couldn't see her face. Her body smelled of grease and flames: blue-crackled, lit, slivered. I smashed the sweater over her blazing head. Crushed the flames, beat at them with the sweater and my hands. I was burning, on fire too. I heard her flesh sizzle, smelled the scorching body. Heat rose, surrounded us. An island of fire. We would die together. It was meant. No way out.

When I came to–only a few seconds later, I think–the fire was out. I was sprawled face down on the floor, my body half-shielding hers. Every bone and muscle ached. My fingers felt as if I'd stuck them inside the blazing kiln and kept them there while flames licked off the layers of flesh. The pain so fierce it snatched my breath.

The smell of burning flesh filled the air. I sat up and looked at her. Shrunken and twisted, the color of charcoal. Her body hard, hot. I turned her over gently and gasped, retched. Her face black. Eyes open as if she stared at me. Eyebrows and lashes singed off. Nose torn at the snout. Ripped off like a piece of clay. Mouth open in an endless scream.

*In the dark and pain, I see God.* A thing that has no face, but that is more beautiful than anything I've ever seen in my life. . . . It penetrates me and carries my spirit to a region over the world. . . . He is everywhere, but can't be seen except in the results of His creation: the sun, earth, stars, men, animals, trees, the sea. He will accompany me to that mansion, I have no doubt. I'll find Him at my side. . . .

—Eugenio-Maria Romero,

*El martirio de la joven Hatchuel o la heroina hebrea,*

Gibraltar, 1837

# *holy sparks*

I STICK MY HEAD INSIDE HIS ROOM. It's so dark I can barely see. I push in the door and step inside. Blueblack shadows drape the walls. To the left, I glimpse his bed, narrow like mine, and a small table. A tall metal armoire. Glints of light shoot from the wall facing me, above the dresser. I take another step in and see my own face–luridly gleaming. He's got the same distorted funhouse mirror as I do in my room.

"What are you doing here?"

I nearly jump, force myself to turn slowly. "I just wanted to see your room."

"Why?"

"Because it's always locked."

"You think I'm hiding bodies here?" He moves to the bed and turns on a small lamp on the table. Yellow, flickering light, not much more than a candle. He drags a large black leather bag from under his bed, opens the tall armoire, and pulls out a handful of shirts.

I sit on the edge of his bed and watch. "Are you planning on moving in with Lydia? What about Sylvie?"

He ignores me, goes to the dresser and brings back under-

74

wear, undershirts, and socks, throws them into the bag next to me. I reach in to grab anything I can, when he turns from the armoire and looks at me. My hand caught deep in his bag. I lift my arm and set my empty hand on my knee. "Why do you always have to go?" I hate the plaintive tone in my voice.

He squints at me. "Lonely?" When I nod, he says, "Go out with Mani."

"I do."

He jerks his shoulder as if to say, what else do you want? Zips the bag shut and sets it on the floor, then sits on the edge of the bed next to me. I'm nearly as tall as he is. Even though he rarely uses this bed, still–we're sitting here together, side by side. I feel a shiver of excitement inside, a giggle that wants to escape. To make sure it doesn't, I give him my most serious, thoughtful look (I call it my Camus look). I need something of his for the spell, can't forget my mission. We're very close to each other. The room is dark. I take a deep breath and try to force my heart to slow its crazy gurgling dance.

"What's with these?" He reaches over and lightly touches a red bird flying across my white knee. "You look about twelve."

"I'm a woman. I'm eighteen."

"You're a big little girl."

"How do you know?"

"I know."

I'm angry but I don't know how to show him he's wrong. "You don't see me."

"No? Tell me what I don't see."

The shadowed room is like a synagogue or church–or what they aim to be: a sacred space. I'm here, inside the forbidden room. It suddenly hits me when I had this feeling before, and the stray giggle bursts out. Smack, in his startled face.

"What's so funny?" He sounds distant and cold, as if he's tuning in from a remote planet. I wish I could grab him and force him to see me here, inches from him.

"I sneaked into the boys' bathroom at school once."

"When boys were in?" That vague weariness of his, completely unshockable.

"No. After school. I went in with my best friend Ti."

"Ti? Was that the one you used to kiss?"

Of all the things to remember about me! That day in Horsens, I had told him about Ti and me. I don't answer, and he turns almost totally around so he's facing me, sucking in his left cheek. "You liked kissing her more than kissing boys. I remember. So what happened in the boys' room?"

"You know what?" My voice rises, "It's not fair! The way boys do it all in a row, while girls hide in stalls–as if we're doing something wrong."

He raises an eyebrow, faintly impressed. "Did it make you feel more like a boy?"

"No. I tried to pee, but it didn't fit my shape."

"Hmm. Did it change anything with Ti?"

"No. We kept on–kissing and stuff–you know. But maybe–I was braver."

## holy sparks

He smiles. And it's so much like Mom in that moment—
glistening teeth against gold-dark skin: exotic, hot, home. All
thoughts of giggles leave me at that moment, and I swallow
and just keep staring at him. He knows. I think he must
know because he sighs and opens his arms and I lean toward him, press my ear against his chest, and feel his arms
close around me. After a minute he rests his chin on the top
of my head. I'm twisted: legs dangling from the bed, upper
part of my body turned toward him, face buried against his
chest. I hear his heart, scatting and thumping—an impenetrable, improvised beat. He smells like Gaby: that wild mix
of sardines and the orange-vanilla potters' soap and dark
spices. His women mingling in it so that his smell is com-
plex, layered. My breathing slows down. I feel easier in my
skin and with him. This is my tonton after all, my family. His
arms around me, his chin resting on my head. For a moment
I can almost believe I'm safe.

He stirs and reaches in the pocket of his black trousers. I
jam my face deeper against his chest, loving the hard, im-
movable feel of him, as if I'm ramming against a mountain.
He shoves a white handkerchief in my face. I blow my nose
hard. His shirt is wet. I didn't even realize I was crying. I
want to apologize but instead find myself telling him about
finding Mom last August. "I ran into the dining room and fell
over her. She was so still—and you know Mom—she was
never still. I used to beg her to stop cooking and cleaning
and putting up wallpaper, but she never did. And suddenly
she was lying on the floor, staring at the ceiling, completely

77

still. But it was all wrong. I wanted her to move–" I catch a ragged breath behind my tongue.

He pushes me away a little, lifts my face so he can see me. I press my cheek back against his chest. I don't want to look at him, or have him look at me.

"Wallpaper hung in strips down the wall. She must have tripped over her little stepladder. She used to carry it from room to room. Every day, year after year, I came home from school and she was papering over another wall. Trellises, roses, watering cans, garden gates–all in these sick pastel colors. Dad and I would look at her and wonder, how many layers of wallpaper will it take to kill memory?"

"It's over now, little cat."

"No, it's not! She was still holding the brush in her hand. I threw myself over her. She was boneless, limp. Wheaty paste all over her fingers. Wind and rain blew in. She always opened the window when she worked, and I smelled the pretzel factory. She called it the fooling smell. She hated it. You think you're at the sea, she told me, but it's only pret-zels."

I push back from him, sit up, and cover my face with the handkerchief, blow my nose again.

"What did you do?"

I look at him out of eyes that can barely see. He's a dark, wet blur. "I knew she was dead. The first time I ever saw a dead person. And it was Mom." I look beyond him to the wall, the shadows like a trellis, a garden gate, as if the wall-paper has moved here, to his room. "I phoned Dad at the market. Then I picked up her stepladder, stood on it, and tore the fucking paper off. Layer after layer. Twelve years of layers. I ripped at it all night. Dad helped me. And still we couldn't get to the source, to where it all began."

I'm crying again, with huge heaving sobs that shake the bed. He says nothing for a while. I feel him watching me. I wanted to cry for so long, and I couldn't, and now at the worst time, it all comes out. I sense someone in the door-way–probably Mama Ledicia zeroing in on me with her radar–and him gesturing for her to go away. And still I cry, until I have no tears left. At least that's how it feels. As if I'm a dried-up river, baked and cracking in the heat.

I use his handkerchief to blot my face and blow my nose again, then take a couple of deep shuddering breaths and look at him: a dark shadow hunched toward me, in a room of shadows. I should be embarrassed. I should get up and go wash my face.

He says in his low, hoarse voice that sounds disembodied in the dark, "Do you remember when you left El Kajda? Sheba and Joseph were packed and ready to go. They had to take the bus to Casablanca, the train to Tangiers, the ferry to Gibraltar, and finally board the ship. And just as they were about to leave, you disappeared. The mellah was still crowd-ed in those days, and for hours, everyone searched for you. Then I had an idea. I came back here, got down on my knees, and guess who I found under my bed?"

"Don't–" I begin, not sure what I mean. Don't shame me, or don't make me cry again, or don't remind me that I've

always been a fool for you, even at the age of six. Don't. Because that means there is no world outside this dark room,
no way out, the window boarded up, the door always
locked—and you hold the key, nowhere to go but back under
your bed, waiting for you to find me.

IT'S AFTER MIDNIGHT WHEN GABY LEAVES for Lydia's house.
As soon as he's gone, and the house is silent again, I wake up
Zahra. We run between the kitchen and the courtyard, two
skinny mice on tiptoe, trying not to wake anyone as we fill
the huge marmite on the low charcoal fire. While we circle
the simmering pot, we chant and throw in spices, herbs,
twigs, Gaby's undershirt (confiscated in my pj's from his
room), the shaving brush, his empty boxes of cigarettes and
matches, and mysterious powders and stones that Zahra
claims are enchanted. I breathe in the ripe-sweet, nearly rotting smell, as if we've entered a Pennsylvania forest in late
fall, with thick, moist humus carpeting the ground. As the
liquid boils, it fills the courtyard sky with billows of vapor. I
repeat Zahra's incantations, pray I'm not asking for the de-
struction of Jews, or the death of anyone. I wish the barrier
of language didn't stand between us. I want to ask her questions, to find out more about her, who she is. "Why?" I ask
her at one point, as we're waiting to begin the fourth round
of circling, whispered chants.

"Why?" she echoes, then gives a sharp nod, head bent to
the right. "I loved, too."

"Where is he?"

Face somber, she slices her throat with her index finger.

"Dead?" I gasp and point to the pot on the fire. "This killed him?"

She almost smiles. "La, la, not this. This, he's mine. After, he die. Sick stomach." I think she says stomach.

"This–" I point to the marmite again– "this won't hurt him?"

"La, la. This, he see only you."

Mani comes in late from the Majestic, smells the bubbling potion and laughs outright. "What did they do to you in America? Take away your brain?" Still grinning, he whirls me around and bends me backwards until my head nearly touches the tiles.

"Stop, you idiot! I need your help."

"Leave me out of this. I'm already spying at the factory for you. Just forget him, Brit. He's out of your league."

"Don't you dare say that!"

"Not to mention that he's your uncle. Do you want to turn into a cliché? One of those mountain girls who marries her uncle?"

"Who's talking about marriage?"

"Well, what do you want? One night? That's not hard. Ask any of the girls in town. Or keep showing up at the port like you did today. He'll get the picture."

I glance over at Gaby's boarded window. "I just want him to see me."

"That's what I'm worried about. When he does see you. If

only it wasn't Gaby, it would be okay. Why don't you go after Tonton Elie?"

Shy Tonton Elie, with his soft flushed cheeks and pursed pink lips. Only a year older than Gaby but at least fifty years older in life-weight. Too shy to ask a woman out. More comfortable with his religious texts and parables. Whenever he sees me, he blushes. He makes me embarrassed—for no reason, for simply existing.

Mani lets go of me, does a split and rises in one easy motion. The only thing marring his grace is the shaggy wig tipping to one side. And the penciled eyebrows. "Help me with Gaby, and I won't sleep until I figure out a way to make the wig stay on your head. And I'll give you my eye pencils to keep. I swear, Mani."

He grips my shoulders. "You don't need him to see you. What you need is to see *him*. When he finishes with Lydia, he's going back to Sylvie. She's waiting for him like a little dog. You should have seen her at the Majestic tonight. It would have made you sick. Why don't women ever want good guys? Luc was there. He asked about you."

"Mani. If you're not going to help, then leave me alone."

He lets go of me and disappears inside without another word. I know I've hurt him but I'm too far gone now.

Zahra hands me a small tin cup. "Your blood. And think about him while."

I move to the corner of the courtyard behind the kitchen under the small palm tree where cats wait for scraps of food. I push down my pajama pants, squat on the ground, pull out my tampon. Close my eyes and wait. Imagine him smiling through the open window at me, hear the murmur the first morning he saw me again when I returned to Morocco, "C'est toi, petite chatte?"–and suddenly I start crying again– or laughing?–as the blood rushes out of me into the tin cup. It trickles over my fingers–just like the beer–onto the ground. I picture Haim with a spotlight aimed at the corner of the courtyard, cats sniffing around me as I squat over a tin cup, not sure whether I'm laughing or crying, but choking on something, unable to see. And he asks, "How did a girl of la famille get into a situation like this?"

The light blinds me. I shade my eyes with my hand. "It's all for love."

"But aren't you ashamed?" Haim's tone is prissy, even more disapproving than usual.

"No." My own voice is clear. I imagine it ringing through the night and waking Gaby in his cottage. He rolls over. The woman with him covers his ears with her hands. But I whisper, Tan ha'buk, I love you. I feel him tremble. And I know he hears me.

It's near dawn when Zahra and I dip the tin cup into the depths of the potion and empty the rest of the pot. We hug and kiss cheeks. In my room, I set the tin cup behind Camus and Proust. As if Camus has been waiting for me, he slips open to a page. I turn on my little light and read: *Here I understand what is meant by glory: the right to love without limits.*

Lying in bed, I reflect on Camus' words. The right to love

without limits, as if love is a privilege, a freedom. The thing I am not permitted.

Sometime in the night, the door to my room opens slowly. My heart pounds. I can't move. Mama Ledicia enters. She bends over me with a stubby candle and murmurs in Arabic. At first I think I'm dreaming, but she sprinkles me with a shower of sparkles. Chanting softly, a singsong prayer, she walks around my bed. As I try to lift myself, I press deeper into the mattress. My tongue is heavy, enormous in my mouth. Wide-eyed, I watch her and I know she's trying to counteract my spell. I fight her magic with all my strength, everything in me. I've got to win. She can't want more than I do. No one wants as much as I do.

LESS THAN AN HOUR LATER, Justine pokes her head in my window and wakes me up to accompany her to the sla. "I thought you'd like to see it without people. In this light, and on Pesach."

Under slits of purple-streaked sky, we walk in the mellah, down a small street I've never seen before. She crouches and photographs a shrunken door on which a spindly gold hand is painted. "Look at this place," she says. "My dark decaying heart. You know where the word mellah comes from? From melh, Arabic for salt. Jews used to have the job of salting the heads of criminals before they were hung and displayed around city walls." She extends both hands. "Here's what I can't figure out. Why do I keep coming back? Why can't I photograph the French? Their lives are passionate, interesting to me. Paris is the center of culture, intellect, philosophy. Why do I insist on returning here?"

"You want to remember?"

"I wish I could forget. But memories are branded into me. I feel as if I'm recreating a world that's dying before my eyes. We've been here in this country for seven centuries, and no one remembers anything! When I look back into our past as Moroccan Jews, it's dark, like the mellah. A dark line, broken by glimpses of sun. A friend from Paris told me once, you come to Morocco to forget. We suffer from a sort of cultural amnesia. We forget what happened to us yesterday, the coming and going of the French, the dynasties of Sultans. A great blur of darkness buries us. I fight it by taking photos of doors and windows and faces."

"I feel that way sometimes, as if I'm glimpsing words and images I should remember for a story I need to tell–but as soon as I try to see them clearly, they disintegrate."

She stops before a small house, with a low brown door. "This is the Bensimon sla. Rabbi Eliahu, the most famous rabbi of the mellah, used to live here. Most of the slas are abandoned now, or transformed into houses where Arab families live. This is one of the few that remains active."

We enter, walk through a small tiled room, and find ourselves in the inner courtyard, roofed over and enlarged by adding onto one of the downstairs rooms. We climb the creaking stairs to the cramped, curtained upstairs balcony that serves as the women's gallery. I smell meat cooking, see bright-colored laundry hanging from one corner. As I pull open the curtain and look down at the main sanctuary, I remember my one and only experience in a sla, about two months ago, when I went with la famille for Purim, right after arriving from the States. As the children's cries and women's gossiping reached a crescendo, I grew more and more frustrated, unable to hear a word of what was going on downstairs in the main sanctuary. I pulled aside the curtain and looked down at the men—a sea of skullcaps—serenely praying. Mamouche tugged at my arm. "You're going to disturb the men! How can they pray with the kids screaming?"

At that moment, Haim turned around and saw me. Broad-faced, nostrils flaring, he shouted, "Silence, women!" Mama Ledicia and Perla pulled me by the skirt and closed the curtain. I fell back in my chair and shut my eyes while the male-to-male bonding with God went on downstairs. I tried to imagine any woman complaining that she couldn't pray to God because she was distracted by the presence of her husband or brother nearby. Never had I felt so far from God and so steeped in sin. I'd stayed away from the sla until now.

There are no gold decorations, no stained glass or embroidered Ark covers, no outward signs that this is a temple, except for the dozen memorial oil lamps hanging from hooks in the ceiling. While Justine photographs the room, the pewlike seats and the lamps, I wander around, trying to feel a sense of awe or mystic truth, but as in the concrete and glass Horsens synagogue, I feel nothing. Less than nothing. I find the one thing I love about the Moroccan synagogue is its name: sla, a spit in the eye of a believer.

When I turned fifteen, Dad finally gave in to Mom's pleading, and on Yom Kippur, we actually went to the Horsens synagogue. The ordeal began at the door, when a member of the Welcoming Committee asked for our tickets, which we'd had no idea we needed. Dad, always prouder than any man has a right to be, turned stiff and furious in an instant. Mom stared helplessly at the Guardian of the Door (an unsmiling American Jew in a three-piece suit). It was left to me to convince the Guardian that we were not spies but only three Jews (lost souls) come to worship on the holiest day of the Jewish year.

"Isn't Yom Kippur the Day of Forgiveness?" I asked. "The Day of Atonement and forgiveness, the day when we are all judged? How can you give a Jew a ticket to pray? On this day of all days, does it make any sense?" Looking into his cold, pale eyes, I recalled one of my father's stories: a man tried to get into the sla to give his friend a message, but it was Yom Kippur, and the sla was completely full. No room for one more. The man pleaded and pleaded with the Fez counterpart of the Guardian of the Temple. "I promise I'll only be a minute. I just have to give him a message. It's urgent!" "Okay," the Guardian finally relented. "You can go in. But don't let me catch you praying."

The Guardian of the Horsens sla had let us in, too, convinced by a burst of the same eloquence that gripped me whenever I saw my parents speechless and impotent in the face of authority. I became a tiger, an enormous cat protecting her cubs. Snarling and cajoling, I refused to leave. My parents accepted my newfound power with equanimity. Dad, fragile yet intimidating, behind folded arms and dark glasses. Mom, eyes watering, rouged cheeks aflame—a schoolgirl being reprimanded. At fifteen, I'd grown taller than both of them and had learned, with some degree of success, to navigate my way through the dangerous streets of America.

When we leave, Justine lights a cigar, throws back her head, and closes her eyes. The smell of her cigar is wonderful: tobacco-rich, fragrant, drowning out the decay. I draw closer to her as we walk across the small square and back down the dark street. She stops abruptly, squints, and focuses her camera on the narrow archway that leads to another small arch. A woman in black passes through and turns her head at that moment, long eyes slanting, as if beckoning to us. "A Chinese box world: door into door into door, no end," Justine murmurs. "I think I'll call this series *Land of the Door.*"

When she lowers the camera, she turns to me. "What's the matter, chérie? You look sad."

"The sla was horrible. Even uglier than the synagogue in the States. I think I hate any holy building. Any place you're supposed to go in and find God. But couldn't they at least make the slas more spectacular? Give them some beauty?"

"You know they were forbidden, under threat of death, don't you? We had to create a place to pray, without the Sultan and his guards realizing what we were doing. So the big families, or the Great Rabbis, the ones who could afford it, set aside a room in their house that became known as the Bensimon sla, or the Amiel sla. If the guards made trouble and destroyed the sla, we picked up and started over in another place."

"It must be in our blood to keep running."

"Another name for survival."

"Mani says the exodus is to Paris, not Israel."

She crooks her arm in mine. "Israel, Paris, New York, what does it matter? We've learned to make our home wherever we go. Every home is borrowed anyway."

"Is Paris home?"

"For now." She smiles. "Come and see my home, sweet Brit. I invite you."

*He called himself Benjamin* and begged me to let him join my caravan. He could not return to Tangiers, he said, everything he'd lived for had been torn from him. We sat in my tent and drank absinthe for hours. Despite the heat, he did not remove his coarse woolen burnoose. Slowly, his story unwound—the way I wished I could unwind the scarves that covered most of his face. He spoke of a sister of unearthly beauty languishing in an underground dungeon in Tangiers. "I wasn't allowed to see her," he told me, "so I disguised myself as a woman, draped and veiled, and the guard, an enormous Sudanese man, let me in. I followed him down a slippery path, through dank, wet air, to the cell. She lay there on the ground"—his voice broke—"they had chained her by the ankles, left her to rot alone in this cave with rats and serpents. She saw me and cried out in joy. Too weak to stand, she crawled to the bars."

I poured him another glass of absinthe. "You left her there?"

"I wanted her to leave in my place, and I'd stay behind in the cell. Or I'd attack the guard so that we could both escape. But she wouldn't listen. She said they would kill me. As if that matters, as if anything matters without her. Suleika, mi corazón, Suleika—"

He wept until he fell asleep, but I stayed awake—the night heavy and profound with the power of absinthe and desert wind—wondering at his tale and how this passionate, heartbroken young man had found his way to my tent. A deeper purpose was at work here. Desert, sky, and Maghreb lunacy made my blood hot and boiling. I leaned forward and pulled back the burnoose, and gently unraveled the winding scarf. He awoke and sat up with a start. Light streamed over his forehead and cheeks as if it could not bear to leave him in shadow. I caught my breath at his radiance. He said nothing, but watched me with eyes black and lustrous as the Maghreb night.

Oh wild God, only You know what burns in my heart!

—Pierre Sitou, *Nuits chaudes du maghreb*, 1836

# *mirage*

The First Question: Why is this night different from other nights?

Why is he different from other men?

THAT NIGHT, THE 2ND OF APRIL, 1969 (or the 14th of nisan, 5729), we gather in the dining room for the Pesach seder. Yawning, Côty and Danny, Mamouche's kids, struggle to keep their eyes open. Papa Naphtali told them one story after another from Scheherazade's Thousand and One Tales to keep them awake until Mama Ledicia had the meal ready. I don't know how I'm going to get through this endless night myself, with its endless lineup of prayers, songs, ritual foods, and glasses of wine. I'm waiting for the moment when we finally move into the salon arabe for tea and sweets. Tonight I am going to put the spell on him. Tonight I am going to make sure that he finally sees me.

The dining room smells of wine and mimosa. Danny and Côty sleepily argue over where to sit while ancient Tata Mazaltov tries out chair after chair, insisting that each one is uncomfortable. Mama Ledicia, Zahra and my aunts bustle back and forth from the kitchen, bringing trays of food and setting them on the white lace tablecloth. Charoseth, Perla's specialty, made with mashed dates, ground walnuts and wine; steaming green soup filled with celery, peas, leeks, scallions, onions and parsley; stuffed artichokes; miniature meatballs steeped in raisins and onions; small round pastelles, potato and meat pies seasoned with vinegar; roasted lamb (ceremonially slaughtered the day before by Rabbi Moshe) fragrant with prunes and almonds. Countless salads, all the ones my mother used to make, and more: oranges and black olives in cumin and olive oil, cucumbers in fresh cilantro, broiled tomatoes and green peppers. And of course, sardines in every conceivable form: ground in patties and cooked in tomato sauce and garlic, fried in omelets, grilled in pungent argan oil from Mogador.

Papa Naphtali, dressed in a white djellabah, sits at the head of the table. Gaby, all in black, faces him from the other end. Sandwiched between Sylvie and Tata Mazaltov, he reads the *Haggadah*, dark curls falling over his eyes, while Sylvie reads him.

Scrunched down near Papy with Mamouche and her kids, I steal morose sips of my wine and look at the faces through the crystal: shimmering facets, diamond cheeks, a glittering eye over a sloshing red-purple sea. Soon we'll get to the Plagues: water turned to blood and locust-blackened skies.

Mani's eye is enormous through the glass. Deep whirling brown. Shy Tonton Elie, laughing behind his hand. A gnarled knuckle. Mamouche's pinched red nostril. Perla's chin, too pointed for her face–but through the crystal, attaining an eerie beauty. Mama Ledicia, not sitting long enough for me to capture her in a facet. Papa Naphtali, blue-veined hand, bony fingers gripping the stem of his glass as he reads aloud from the *Haggadah*. I move slowly around the table. Light blinds me. I lift my eye from the glass and see Gaby's eye, pressed against his glass. I lower my glass. He lowers his. Twists his mouth to one side, so far his smile is in the center of his cheek. Grotesque! And then I remember.

The first moment I saw him, four years ago, standing in our living room on the corner of Candlestick and Wise. A pirate in pea coat and jeans, blown in from the sea. He smiled at me. And everything happened at once, but I could grasp only his smile, his ocean eyes, and the shock as he reached to hug me. I stepped back. It was too much. Hurt flashed in his eyes, then he held out his hand to shake mine. We shook hands a long time until I saw the mischievous light in his eyes, the cheek sucked in, and I knew he was playing with me. I shook back even harder, and he grinned. "Ma petite chatte, life is unjust. I've been carrying you in my pocket all these years, and now here you are, shot up high as a giant. An Amazon."

I made a face, and he said, "Don't twist your face like that, or I'm going to do pipi on your head!" He leaned closer. "Didn't your mother tell you what happened to Miriam Mendoza?"

"Who's that?" asked Mom. "One of your old girlfriends?"

"I have no old girlfriends. Miriam Mendoza made faces–just like that–at her uncle. A wonderful man. Kind. Patient. Even brilliant. But did she appreciate him? No! Instead she made a terrible face, just one time too many." He twisted his mouth to the center of his cheek, like Clutch Cargo, the cartoon character: tiny pulsing red lips moving on the side of his face. "The next morning she woke up and her mouth was frozen, stuck there. And she wasn't the only one. Did you hear what happened to Madame Amzellag? The one who lived in the villa by the Jardins Publiques? She fell asleep on the sand one day, for at least six hours. When she woke up, it was night. She made her way home in the dark, turned on the light, looked in the mirror–and screamed. Her mouth"–he shut his eyes briefly–"her mouth was twisted to one side. And the same thing happened to Reina Mallul. She had an uncle too."

I found my voice. "It's not true."

"You doubt me?"

"A whole town–with their mouths to one side–" a giggle broke out. "It can't be."

"It can't be," he echoed mournfully. "What have you done to my cat, Sheba? Only fourteen and already ruined."

He danced with my mother, made both my parents laugh with stories about El Kajda. Each story began grimly but soon took a surreal turn. "Remember Isaac Amar? Dead. They tried to make it look like natural causes." He lowered his voice. "I'm sure his wife murdered him."

Mom sputtered, half-laughing. "Gaby! He was over ninety when we left! And that was eight years ago!"

"He was only ninety-nine. But in perfect health. Don't worry. I'll investigate when I get back." His face was elastic, endlessly mobile, with a wide mouth and eyes that glinted with laughter even when he wasn't smiling. I watched the play of light and shadow across his face: unshaven cheeks, a small valley in the center of his lower lip, a faint dimple in the chin. He was *here*–glowingly alive, laughing, aware–but also *there*–as if he were the hero of my latest saga of dreams: the blue man with whom I soared through the universe.

I tried to see us with his eyes. Frail Dad, two silver-black wings of hair. Mom, a lush fruit bursting from its skin. Hennaed waves of hair, strong and graceful hands. Me, tall, gawky, shy. The food–twenty courses all served at once, as usual. The thick layers of wallpaper. The gold and black globe of the world reflected in the window. I wanted to speak, impress myself on his memory, make sure he wouldn't forget me, but all I could do was rest my chin in my hand and stare at him. I was lost–long before the meal was over and he led me outside and said with a wicked smile, "Alone at last, little cat." Long before that.

Ma nishtana ha'lila hazeh mi kol ha'leilot? Mamouche's kids sing out.

I move my mouth to the left as far as it will go. He laughs aloud. Everyone turns to look at him. I lower my eyes demurely to my *Haggadah*.

The Second Question: Why do we eat bitter tonight?

Why don't I know the difference between bitter and sweet?

AFTER THE MEAL, I OFFER TO MAKE THE TEA. Only Mama Ledicia gives me a dark, suspicious look. Haim is loudly approving: "Now you're behaving like a woman, Brit. Doesn't it feel natural and good?"

I tear leaves from the stalks of mint growing fresh and wild along the wall in the courtyard, bring them in and wash them. When the water in the pot boils, I set in heaping spoonfuls of green tea to brew and squeeze in a few drops of orange-blossom water, Papa Naphtali's secret ingredient for fragrant, sweet tea. I dash to my room to grab the tin cup and luckily make it back to the kitchen without encountering anyone.

I enter the salon arabe with my brass tray of small painted tea glasses. The women, tropical birds, flutter past in black fringed shawls, arms fleshy, white, heavy—except for Justine, who saunters in, wearing a pale gray man's suit with fitted jacket and loose trousers, maroon silk tie knotted at her neck. The air is rich with mimosa, jasmine, sweet mint leaves. The men—Papa Naphtali and my uncles and cousins—gleaming and vital, supremely confident—sit back on the gold divans and watch Perla, Mamouche and Zahra carry in trays of Pesach sweets: alcamonias, walnut and meringue cookies, candied grapefruit peels, dates stuffed with almond paste, sugared balls of crème de marron, and my favorite, mahjoun.

The discussion is still going strong from dinner: to leave

Morocco, or to stay. Jews are not permitted to take their money out of the country. Papa Naphtali cannot leave at his age and start anew, but he wants to plant the dream of Israel for the rest of the family. He holds up a translucent blue-veined hand. Seated cross-legged on the thick red Berber carpet, in his snow-white djellabah, pointed hood casting shadows behind his head, he looks like a Prophet of old: fierce black eyes, flame-lit white froths of hair, mustache, beard. "A prayer for Israel. May our enemies leave us alone. May God protect Israel, our Holy Land. And may all of you here get to set foot on the sacred soil. I want you to dig out the earth of Israel with your fingers, and hold it in your hands, and know it is alive, that it was alive when Solomon walked there, and that David dug his pebbles out from it. I want you to breathe it in, my children, and tell me how it smells and feels. Next year in Jerusalem!"

"Why do we always say next year in Jerusalem?" asks Mani, sprawled on the carpet. "Why not this year?"

Tonton Elie lifts his head from a prayer book. "The time is not ripe yet."

Perla shakes her head. "Elie thinks we have to wait for the Messiah to arrive and give us a sign. Do you know that when the Zionists went to the Berber villages in the mountains and told the Jews about Israel, the villages emptied overnight? The next morning the Berbers searched the villages and couldn't understand how the Jews could leave like that, in a second, give up everything they'd ever known, for a land they'd never seen."

"A land they'd never seen but that they knew in their bones," says Papy.

Elie shrugs. "I know that we'll all eventually end up in Israel. It's the only place we'll ever feel at peace."

"At peace!" cries Haim. "Are you crazy? Where farmers carry guns and we're surrounded by enemies. War there is a jihad. Did you hear what they said in '67? Killing Jews is a holy mission, and the more Jews you kill, the sooner you get to Allah."

"Why not move to Paris?" asks Justine.

"Since when do the French love Jews?"

"No one loves us but at least I don't live in fear."

"I'll tell you who loves us!" shouts Haim, slapping his broad chest. A vein throbs over his bushy eyebrow and his nostrils are flared. He looks on the verge of exploding. "King Hassan loves us and has sworn to protect us."

King Hassan II. His photo is plastered on every wall in every office, store and building I've entered in Morocco, including the sardine factory. Zahra touches his photo hanging in the entrance hallway to my grandparents' house and brings her fingers to her lips—for protection and good luck—the way everyone in la famille kisses the mezuzah at the front door (a green and black ceramic piece carved by Gaby) when entering or leaving the house. Every time I see Hassan II's unsmiling but oddly benign face, I remember Dad telling me how he went skating once on a mountain lake in Ifrane. Mohammed V, the father of Hassan, the future king, was there, skating with his two bodyguards. Whenever he slipped, the bodyguards had to fall too.

Justine fights Haim all the way—as does Gaby, when he can be bothered to respond. They both argue that it isn't until you leave Morocco that you realize you've been on your knees all your life.

Mani says, "I work with Arabs all day at the factory. Sometimes a whole day goes by, even two, and we're just people, brothers, doing our work, laughing at the same jokes. Then the news comes on the radio. Someone mentions Israel, and the mood turns ugly. Eyes that were friendly a minute ago watch me. Most Jews I know won't even go into work whenever anything happens in Israel. How long can we live with that kind of fear?"

Justine says, "Doesn't the fact that there are no teenagers in the mellah mean anything to you? At age twelve all the kids are shipped off to Paris or Lucerne. You're fools to stay. You don't want Mani working in a factory where he can't feel safe for the rest of his life, do you? Or Côty and Danny to grow up the way we did?"

"I want to be free!" says Mani. "To feel completely free. To walk in a land that's mine. Not a land that *suffers* me."

"Don't kid yourself," says Haim. "Israel will suffer you too. The Jews from Germany and Eastern Europe see us as Arabs, not Jews. They don't want us any more than the French do."

So where is home for this family?

## THE ROAD TO FEZ

BENDING OVER THE LOW, ROUND BRASS TABLE in the center of the room, I set down the tray of glasses—already poured (I'm just waiting for Haim to shout, *That's not the way we do it here, Brit!*). I look at the brass key in its place of honor, a shrine to the past. Do they seriously think they'll ever go back to Spain?

"Why not America?" I suggested earlier at the seder.

Gaby said, "Why? So we can all turn out like you and forget what we are? What did you call yourself? A Christian from Paris? Or was it a Hindu from India?"

The attack stunned me. Everyone laughed. He smiled at me, the same mocking smile as when he spilled beer on me—and later pretended it was a joke.

The discussion rages on while I pass out the glasses of tea, beginning with Papa Naphtali. He takes the tea from me and motions for me to crouch so he can put his hand on my head and murmur a prayer over me.

Tata Mazaltov complains loudly that the tea is cold while Perla shushes her, "She's doing her best."

Mani shakes his head and whispers, "Tonight I'm dragging you to the Majestic. Don't even think about staying here and mooning over him."

I try not to meet anyone's eyes. Even though I haven't looked at Gaby once since I entered the salon arabe, I know exactly where he is and what he's doing. Sitting back on one

100

of the gold divans while Sylvie leans toward him, playing with his hair. He's been too busy listening to her whisper in his ear to participate in the latest discussion.

I am suddenly angry at myself for the spell, for everything. Mani is right: I am a total idiot. I had a boyfriend in the States. Even though Mom hated Sun God ("He's a man of props," she said, "take away the guitar, the long hair and scarves and velvets, and there's nothing there"), we got high, laughed and made love. Maybe I should head back home, go to college, forget the Suleika bullshit, break free from this pattern. The stupid brass key on the wall. I'm sure they think it's noble and aristocratic: their pure faith that one day their home in Spain will be restored to them. I find it blind, self-defeating. So that instead of packing their bags and getting the hell out of here, they sit in this lush gold room and discuss the options to death.

I throw Gaby a filthy look. Easy for you to criticize my Dad and me. The courage it took for him to wrench himself from the only world he'd ever known, the safety and security of his family, and travel to America with his wife and daughter. Not speaking a word of English, no hoard of money to tide us over. He took a job in a supermarket packing meat and began taking me on field trips to downtown Horsens. At thirteen, I was already his height. We both walked with our hands fisted in our pockets. He wore his eternal dark glasses, his long, fine, gray-streaked black hair shielding his thin cheeks. Did we look like Christians from Paris?

He led me down Liberty Bell Road to the church I'd attended with my dreaded enemies, Bobby and Helen Kratzer, gnome-apprentices to Mrs. Kopf, the dreaded djinn. Dressed in Moroccan finery, a too-long green velvet dress hand-sewn by Mom, I sat at a desk, sandwiched between the twins who examined me the entire time to see if I betrayed myself. The Sunday School teacher, Mrs. Donahue, false teeth quivering, half falling out of her mouth with emotion, exclaimed, "Welcome this little lost lamb to the fold! You have a friend in Jesus, Brit! The Kratzers tell me you're a Jew! Well, we all have our problems!"

Dad and I stared at the facsimile of the cracked bell on the church's tiny front lawn. "Freedom," I said before he could ask. "The land of the free. That's why we came to America."

"But even here, they don't know us." The bitter voice grated through me as I watched his silver-lit hair blow back in the wind. "I'll never forget how they looked at me when we first arrived. The president of the only synagogue in Horsens, with no more than fifty members, asked me, 'Did you ever hear of the Torah in Morocco?' Me! Raised to be a rabbi!" He breathed hard, shoved his hands back in his pockets. "He told me: 'You're better off going back to the jungle in Africa. There's no place for you here.' Not one of them offered to help us find a job or a place to live. Not one of them even offered me a cup of coffee! I didn't ask them for a penny. I didn't ask for a damn thing!"

I couldn't look at him at that moment. I felt shamed, en-raged. I didn't know what to do with my hands. "But I don't want to be a Christian from Paris." My voice low, a mumble.

"Bobby and Helen Kratzer already know, and they tell everyone, and they all make fun of me."

Dad took off his dark glasses and rubbed his eyes. The sight of them–green-brown, narrowed, naked to the gray light–always gave me a start. "What do you want? This?" He smelled his hands, then thrust them from him. "I stink of meat! Am I killing myself at the supermarket, packing beef and chicken in freezers every day, every night, so you can become like your mother and her sainted idiot, Suleika, and–" He broke off. "Sheba tells you that Suleika is your second mother. Well, I'm going to tell you about your grandmother. *My* mother."

"Dad–" His eyes were pinpoints of light, his hands still out in the open.

"Picture this, Brit. And don't forget it." His voice shook. "In 1912, when the French were about to take over Morocco, they ordered everyone–Jews and Arabs–to give up their weapons. The Jews–dummies as always–handed theirs in. But the Arabs of Fez were angry at the French. Do you know how they showed their anger?" He paused, thin lips gritted tight. "They held onto their weapons and stormed through the mellah for three days. Three days, Brit. They looted and burned the houses. And they killed every Jew they found." He jerked his thin wrist. "They called it the Fez Massacre. To distinguish it from other massacres." He jerked his wrist again, more sharply. "My mother was a girl then, a kid. She hid under a table and watched the Arabs shoot her parents and brother. When the killers left, she ran down the stone street through pools of blood filled with human bones."

I clenched my hands so tightly in my jacket pockets that my fingernails cut into my palms.

"She ran past hills of corpses to the Sultan's Palace right outside the mellah. The Sultan was a good man. When he realized that his people were wiping out the entire mellah, thousands of Jews, he decided to help save those of us who were left. You know what he did?" Dad leaned closer to me, so close our noses almost touched. His face was concentrated in fury. I smelled the raw meat he'd complained of—and more: I smelled his rage—pure, undiluted. The sky darkened. The cracked bell in front of us looked grubby and grimy, a pale imitation of the genuine bell in Philadelphia.

"He opened the gates to the cages of his menagerie in the courtyard, where he kept exotic, wild animals. And the Jews filed in. Can you see my mother? A little girl, cowering in a cage next to pumas, tigers and leopards, but safer *there* than in the street." He made a soft, spitting sound. "The Sultan's zoo: beasts and Jews. *That's* what I see when I hear the word Jew."

I closed my eyes and saw my grandmother Alice in a cracked yellowing photograph: a long-nosed, dour-faced, kerchiefed woman. Behind her weary eyes, I saw the orphaned girl who ran down a bloody street to a cage. The cage was crowded, filled with barefoot Jews in black, lamenting and wailing to their invisible God. I saw Suleika, black eyes glinting with tears, as she shook the bars. The cage was packed to bursting with wild animals and Jews.

Sardines in a can, they slid over each other, trying to find a firm grip.

Dad gripped my arm hard. I opened my eyes, and with a shock, saw he was crying, tears covering his thin cheeks in an instant. Fierce, trembling, he whispered, "Now do you understand? I'm setting you free from that cage."

Papa Naphtali's raspy voice sounds through the walls and veils of memory, "And so, why is this night different from all other nights?" *I miss you, Dad. How are you managing alone, without Mom and me?* I look down at the two remaining glasses on the tray: Gaby's and Sylvie's. Wish I could just spill them out and start over. From the beginning. From the moment I was born.

The Fourth Question: Why do we recline on this night?

Why not turn and run instead, back to safety?

"THIS IS WHAT PESACH MEANS TO ME," says Papa Naphtali. "It represents the most courageous, terrifying decision human beings have ever made, to leave a known life of slavery, and to enter the unknown, dangerous promise of freedom. They had to lose the habits of slavery, to learn to straighten their shoulders and to look strangers directly in the eyes. It took forty years of wandering in the desert before the last generation born as slaves was gone, and the first generation born free and wild in the desert was ready to fight for the promise. Imagine the terror. Imagine looking over the rocks into the land you thought was a myth, and seeing that it was real, that you could touch the ground and smell the air. We're always on the verge of freedom, but frightened to take that last step. So what will we do, mes enfants? Remain in the desert for another forty years? Or advance to the vision of light, which may be a mirage?"

Holding the last two small glasses, I trudge through the prickling, harsh desert, the Berber carpet digging into my bare feet. The Gaby-glass is so full it sloshes. I imagine it burning through the carpet and Sylvie shrieking, Oh my God, we're being poisoned!

I thrust the glass of tea at Sylvie's delicate heart-face. The pale blue eyes, bloodshot, weary. Even the miracle of kohl can't camouflage the strain of being Gaby's official fiancée.

"Merci, Breet," she breathes in her tiny voice.

I hold out his glass. For the longest time he doesn't take it—until I'm forced to meet his eyes. Angry at me. Again. But he's smiling, pretending he's not mad. I feel like grabbing the glass back and spilling it over him. I don't care if you are my uncle, or that I love you. Right now I hate you.

"Is this Brit's special?" He takes a sip and nearly gags. His whole face twists into an unholy grimace. I look down quickly. Study the movement of wrist to hand. The way the long olive fingers clasp the small glass—and then I see the bumps and ridges along the lengths of the fingers. The withered, bubbled dark caps of flesh covering each fingertip, slashing like arrows to the knuckles.

"What the fuck is in this tea?"

I am frozen, one of Justine's photos, caught in a time-warp. Staring at the scarred hands before me. The man slowly coming into focus: achingly real. Stay a dream–please! Stay my blue man. The one who explored my room that night in Horsens and who refused to leave even though Mom yelled that the cab was here, waiting for you. Instead you sat on my bed, your face blue-shadowed from the neon 17 REASONS WHY, and asked, "Seventeen reasons why what?"

"I don't know," I said. "Why to eat pretzels I guess."

"Or why it's so hard to go."

I sat up under the covers. "Tell me one."

"I'll tell you two. Your eyes. I could drown in there if I wasn't careful."

"You're a sailor," I said, suddenly brave. "You know how to swim."

"Sailors drown, little cat."

Mom yelled, "Gaby!" and I threw my arms around you and pressed my face against the hollow of your throat. I was hot, burning, shivering. I held onto you as hard as I could but already you were slipping away–the way a dream does, no matter how hard you try to keep it still, intact, undiminished.

A burned hand shoves the glass back at me. Empty. He drank every last drop. Amazed, I look at him: still shuddering, wiping his mouth with the back of his wrist. The palm of his hand is bleached, the flesh dried, gathered into narrow folds of skin.

"Now what happens?" He holds out both hands to me. The right one doesn't flatten but stays slightly curved. "Do my hands miraculously heal?"

107

The flush rises from my throat up my cheeks to my fore-head. I want to sink into the carpet. Sylvie watches me curi-ously, still dainty-sipping her tea.

He leans closer. "Or is it a different kind of spell? Do I suddenly begin fondling you in front of my girlfriend and parents?"

BEHIND ME, PAPA NAPHTALI SAYS, "Time circles and returns to that endless moment in the desert. For the Jews, it's al-ways that moment. For us, it's always now."

We all hold up our glasses and drink and laugh and try to hold back the morning.

*What do we see from below?* You think that because we're the under-side of the city, squatting over the vats of dyes and pigeon shit and cow piss, that we can't see beyond all of you looking down at us through binoculars and cameras, mint leaves pinched to your noses? Well, Monsieur Ficelle—Mister String!—I saw a saint. You don't believe me. No one else is alive from those days to bear me witness. But ask yourself this, Monsieur Parisien, why would I lie? If I dreamed her, then why not say I dreamed the years in the Souk Dab-baghin, leaping from vat to vat, dipping the skins in indigo, poppy, mint and saffron? The stains that never wore off my fingers and feet? The rotting stink of goat, sheep, cow and camel skins that made my wife turn away from me in disgust? Have it your way. I never saw Lalla Suleika clutching the bars of her cell at the Prison Sidi-Fraj as I walked to and from the Chouara. Three days the Sultan kept her in that tiny cell facing the square. Guards stood by, making sure no one killed her. We all knew she was an infidel, one who swore to fol-low the laws of Islam, and later turned her back on the true faith. She was a whore, everyone said. She deserved to die. The Aissaouwa, wearing wild beast skins, marched in a frenzy through the Square Bab-Dekaken to her cell. They smashed their skulls with chains until blood poured down their faces and bod-ies. One of them bit into a live sheep, tore it apart with his hands and teeth, and shoved the heart through the bars.

I was a newlywed, stained yellow and red up to my elbows, not yet know-ing how the dye would eat away at my wife's desire, how she would grow to hate me, how my sons would abandon the tanner's trade, one after the other, how I'd be left alone in the tanner's square, under the roof of hundreds of stretched and beaten skins, wondering what had gone wrong.

I walked through the square, avoiding the mob that gathered at her cell, the stones and eggs they pelted her with. What had she to do with me? An in-fidel, in two days no longer one of the living. But on the third and last day *before her execution, something drew me to her. I pushed through the crowd. The guards tried to control the people but they were enraged, spitting and cursing her. An old woman threw a shoe at her. It almost hit my head. I pushed my way through until I was so close I saw her knuckles. Sore and chapped as mine, pinched white. She'd been gripping those bars a long time. Her eyes stared through me as if I didn't exist, as if none of us did. And then I knew why Allah had sent me here, to her cell. I needed to have her eyes meet mine. She needed to know I existed. Why, I wasn't sure, but she had to see me. I touched her hand lightly. She jumped and blinked. Then she saw me. Only me. She stared, her black eyes burning holes through my flesh until I was a skin hanging to dry under the sun. She saw everything, everything, and I let her see it, every bit of my sorry life and lonely nights and dreams. I knew in a second the healing would begin. I knew it as sure as I feel your camera on me.*

*Well, the guards saw me there and dragged me from her. I screamed like I never screamed in my life, You're making a terrible mistake! Let me go! But they kicked me, and the crowd must have thought I was a djinn with my painted stink, and they kicked and beat me. I didn't go to watch them kill her. How could I? They'd already killed her in me. I've been dead since that day. But not a day passes that I don't go to her tomb in the Jewish Cemetery and light a candle. What do I ask for? Only for her to come back. To please come back.*

—Mudani bn'Thami,
interviewed in
*Fès, Ville Ancienne et Secrète,*
documentary by Armand Ficelle,
1953

# the rider and the sea

CINDERELLA'S TEARS WATERED THE TREE that was her mother. If I cry hard enough, Mom, will the prince on horseback become real?

I rip the black shawl from the window and let the night enter me, sweep through me. Mom, don't leave me alone. Please come back. Sing me "Le rêve bleu" the way you used to. Keep out the sounds of the dark with the blue dream, sing away the djnoun, hold me. Come back, Mom.

WHEN THE FAMILY IS TUCKED SAFELY in their bedrooms, on this night that is different from all other nights, I climb the narrow spiral of stairs to my grandfather's roof terrace. I need help–from above. The moment I open the red and blue stained-glass door, I enter a world that obeys laws of another universe, where time doesn't pass: it remembers, and moves back, forward, and sideways–all at the same time. Six-year-old Brit waits for me there, and I know Papa Naphtali is playing his oud, smoking and thinking. As far as I know, he never sleeps.

Sure enough, he's seated cross-legged on his little tasseled

111

carpet. He plucks strings on the oud, immediately transporting me to the Sahara, a hot sirocco blowing sand over us. He acknowledges my presence with a few mournful chords, then returns to his music. Hypnotic and haunting, his music has no recognizable beginning or end: variations on a theme, examined from every possible angle, until I want to scream, and instead find myself tapping my foot, swaying my head back and forth–waiting for the note to pierce the inner heart.

I sprawl on my belly on the bright white chalk floor and stare at the toenail moon. Forbidden to stare at the moon, I know, from Mom's countless warnings. But I've done other more forbidden things, so why stop now? I can't see the empty brass cages, the fish in their aquarium, the roses, geraniums and carnations growing on bushes along the low stone walls that enclose the terrace. I catch only glints of the arched entrance to a roofed area, where he keeps his sacred texts in Aramaic, Hebrew and Arabic–and his own tales and poems. But their presence surrounds me and makes me feel at peace.

Maybe Dad was wrong to take me away from this–my grandfather, my family. For years, on the forms they gave us at school, I wrote under Religion: *none*, and Birthplace: *nowhere*. A no one, born nowhere, who followed no gods. Is that freedom? But what is the alternative? To never leave home? To always stay in the place you were born, surrounded by people just like you?

The oud stops in the middle of one of its melancholy journeys. Papa Naphtali says, "Do you remember how you used to follow Gaby here? After every visit, I twined a rose around your ear. You pressed the flower against your hair and left a trail of petals down the stairs." I feel his smile in the dark. "Ah Brita, did you know I named you?"

"Mom said Brites was a family name," I mumble against the floor.

"In a manner of speaking. That was how we got it past your father. Brites Henriques was one of your ancestors. Didn't Sheba tell you her story?"

"I know. She died in the Inquisition."

"But how, Brita? How did she die? Like Suleika, my dear, another one for whom life is more than mere existence."

I sit up and hug my knees, facing Papa Naphtali. He glows white, head to toe, like an angel in the dark—or the way I imagine an angel.

"She was about your age. The brown hoods of the Inquisition were spying everywhere, seeking out hidden Jews, trying to sniff us out. A neighbor betrayed the Henriques family, swore she saw them wash on Fridays. A sure sign they were preparing to welcome the Sabbath bride. Jews! The Inquisitioners came to the Henriques house and arrested the entire family. They marched the family to the court, while neighbors jeered and shouted. The louder they shouted, the more they hoped to make themselves invisible to the restless eyes of the Inquisitioners.

"The trial began.—Are you Jews?—No.—Why do you wash yourselves on Fridays?—We want to be clean.—Why do you lie?— We're not lying.—Who are you protecting?

"On trial for hiding the fact that they are Jews in a land that has exiled all its Jews and killed the rest. There is no way out alive once you've reached the court. The family knows this. The youngest one, the girl Brites, watches the court sentence her father, her mother, her brothers and older sister, her aunt and uncle. But the court isn't happy. They want more Jews to kill. They demand more names. They are given none.

"The torturers begin and continue until the whole family is burned alive. Everyone, except Brites. It's not mercy in the court. It's—maybe a moment of hesitation. A fraction of a second. That quickly passes. But they don't burn her like the others. They bring her before the court—the last survivor of the Henriques clan—and demand more names, a confession, words to erase the smell of fire and burned flesh. She faces the scorching eyes of the Inquisitioners and sings the song of Pesach:

*Adonai, Adonai!*

*Adonai, my Lord*

*Let us sing today to the Lord*

*Of that singular hour,*

*The horse and the rider*

*He threw into the deep sea.*

"They shave her head and lock her in a convent. Jewess, they tell her, you will become a bride of Christ. The next morning she is found hanged in her cell." Papa Naphtali clears his throat. "I hoped you would have her courage."

"I don't, Papy. I'm a coward. And I do stupid things. And

everyone sees through me. But I see nothing. Nothing at all."

"What didn't you see tonight?" I watch the leaves, barely trembling. "That he was with his fiancée? That he is scarred–"

"Oh God, Papy."

"–not only his hands, but in his mind and heart?"

"Am I transparent? What's happened to me here? It's as if my flesh were ripped off and I'm just a naked hungry heart." A long deep sigh shakes through me.

"Now that sigh contains centuries of sorrow and pain. What's wrong, Brita? Do you think we haven't all been there–or worse? Do you think you're alone in love?"

"I know you're going to warn me how stupid I'm being, how dangerous it is, how he's off limits to me."

"Don't tell me what I'm going to say. I'd rather say it myself, if you don't mind."

"Okay." My voice as sullen and ungracious as I feel. A clod of lumpy earth in this airy paradise.

"Many years ago I was invited to a cousin's wedding in Casablanca. It was a summer house-party lasting two weeks before the wedding. Weddings were big productions in those days, the merging of two families, and they often lasted weeks with guests coming from the entire country. The first day I arrived, I ran into my cousin and his bride-to-be. Now, I've always been a dreamer, Brita. Like you. Like Gaby. And no one falls like a dreamer. I looked at this girl, as fierce and beautiful as a lioness, and my past disappeared, my present was meaningless, and my future only a way to get to her."

"The bride? You fell in love with the bride?"

"I did."

"What happened?"

"I had two weeks in which to convince her that I was the man of her dreams. Immediately I faced an almost insurmountable problem: this woman had left her dreams far behind. I had to remind her what dreams were, and then to superimpose myself on the dream, so that when she woke up, she saw my face, heard my voice."

"Didn't you wonder if you were doing something wrong? Interfering in fate? I mean, she was supposed to marry someone else."

"You're asking how I knew. She was my holy spark. Hard and sharp-edged. She glowed in the dark."

"Like you."

"Aah." He sounds delighted. "Now here's the thing with holy sparks. They are necessary of course, we need to gather them to return to the Promised Land, but they don't come announced, or gift-wrapped, or labeled. You trip over them and see them glittering in the dirt. When you find your holy spark, you grab it and hold tight. They fight you to the death. They don't want to be caught. But you hang on–"

The door opens behind me. I don't turn, but my heart catches in my chest. It can only be Tonton Elie or Gaby

"Oh, you're not alone. I'll come back later." Gaby's disappointed voice.

"Sit," says Papy. "It's like old times, the three of us up here."

116

"I hate to disappoint you Papa, but time does pass. It's not the same. We're all older, if not wiser." I hear him sit on the floor behind me.

"Why did you come tonight, mon fils? There must be movement and turbulence in the planets tonight. We are troubled. None of us can sleep."

"I feel like hell. My stomach is killing me." He kicks me in the butt. "Thanks to Brit and her tea."

"Why did you drink it?" Papy asks.

The crack of a match. I hear his indrawn breath as he inhales. "I don't know. Because I'm a fool. Maybe it's a good thing you're up here, Brit. I want you to leave me alone. No more coming to the factory, or to my room, no more spells. Do you hear me?"

Tears sting my lashes, spark in my eyes. "I'm sorry. I was just going to tell Papy that it's time for me to leave."

"Leave El Kajda? Morocco?" Gaby's voice so sharp it pricks my flesh like thorns.

"I'm going to Fez to see Suleika." As soon as I hear the words, I know that it is the right thing–the only thing–to get me out of this coil.

"It's truly a shame," says Papy. "We–la famille–put you both on guard. Despite the age difference, you were always friends."

"It's no one's fault but mine. I was pushing where I didn't belong. Mom always said I was a trespasser."

"Everyone with any intelligence is a trespasser. I am one, too. I've taken the roof–which is the woman's world–and made it mine. Gaby is a trespasser, aren't you, my son? Going from the port to the pôterie to the mellah. Suleika was one, too, you know. She crossed from the Jewish world to the Arab world. In those days there was no mellah in Tangiers, but still the separation was distinct, an invisible wall. I used to wonder how long it takes to cross from the Jewish house to the Arab house. An eternity. Or a second. A breath, and you're there, in the other world."

Gaby says, "I had a dream once in which I counted the steps between the Jewish house and the Arab house. There were twenty-two."

Papy nods. "And when you're there, you look around and realize you're in the same house, even the same room. The only difference is that you've entered from another door. But that is enough to change everything."

"The first time I realized that we were all in the same room was at the pôterie when Tuhami told me Suleika's story. Not the version I knew, about the little saint. It was the same girl, but another story created around her. When he finished telling me, I looked at the pieces we were working on, side by side, different but the same. Do you know what I mean? Of course you do. That was when everything changed for me, with the clay. I knew that if the story has to be real to everyone in the room—no matter which door they come through—then I have to give them openings, entrances—"

"Breathing space," I say.

He hesitates, then nods. "Exactly. We're all in that same room, and we all have to breathe."

"Tell us Tuhami's story," says Papy.

"You're the storyteller."

"Tell the story."

As Gaby speaks, I picture the slits he carved in his enormous vessels, the mirror inside the one in the salon arabe, as if to say to the viewer, "Hey you, looking in, you're part of this too." And I see Mom's Suleika: a second mother, the saint whose tomb she had hugged as if it were a living, breathing woman, and the certitude she'd had upon leaving the cemetery that Suleika had given her a child. "You'll always be connected to Suleika," Mom told me. "When I read the tea leaves and see you creeping under the shadows, she is in the curl of the leaf, watching over you."

"She was a bad girl," says Gaby. "Like someone I know. Her mother was a jealous bitch who couldn't stand the sight of her. When she laughed, her mother wanted to shut her up. When she dreamed about the future, her mother swore there wouldn't be one. But Suleika was no angel. She knew her mother hated her, and she figured, I can't do anything right anyway, and whatever I do, I get beaten, so I might as well do what I want. She got into trouble every day, hung around with the Arabs. In Tangiers, Jews and Arabs lived side by side, but still, there was the wall–always the wall–between them. It was dangerous for Jews to try to break through. Only someone as hungry as Suleika would take the chance. Once you crossed over to the other side, you were in their hands–completely. The risk was the only thing that made her feel alive. By the time she turned seventeen, she was hard and bitter. She'd been beaten so hard and so often it left her numb. She didn't care about anything anymore. Then her mother sold her in an arranged marriage to a sixty-year-old widower with six kids. Ugly as a sardine, with bulging eyes and a red nose that dripped snot down his shirt.

"At seventeen, she was old for a bride in those days. An old maid. Like Brit. The wedding was coming closer and closer. She got wilder. There was only one thing that kept her going. In the evenings, she sat in her courtyard and listened to the music that came from the courtyard next door, where an Arab family lived. She heard the sound of an oud, and a man's voice, singing in Spanish or Arabic, sometimes just humming the melody. The music made her cry. It made her dream. One night, about a week before her wedding, her mother beat the hell out of her. She used a broom, a leather belt, everything she could lay her hands on.

"Crying, Suleika ran to the courtyard. The music was coming from next door. She went to the stone wall, feeling with her fingers for a hole. She saw a gap in the wall, where a stone had fallen out, and looked through. Taleb sat cross-legged, the oud across his lap, strumming it like a guitar. His eyes were closed, and he was singing. This was the first time she'd really seen him. He'd been away at boarding school. When he was home, he didn't go out with the others; instead, he spent his time playing music in the courtyard. He was about her age, good-looking, but different, very quiet. Every day after that, she watched him. I want this boy, she thought. I'm going to play with him. But her plan backfired.

One day she whispered his name through the hole in the wall, and he saw her. He came to the wall and stared at her for a long time. Did I tell you she was beautiful? So beautiful that without saying a word, she left him dazzled and broken. He turned and went back in his house. She stood there, unable to move. That night he sang a new song. She pressed her face against the hole in the wall and watched him. Every string he strummed vibrated inside her. When he finished, he came to the wall and touched her face with the same fingers that had played through her. 'That was for you,' he said. 'From now on, they'll all be for you.'

"After that, it was impossible to stay in her old life. Her mother's beatings, the old dripping widower. She begged Taleb to run away with her. He was engaged to marry, too. Another arranged marriage. He'd never seen the bride, but it didn't matter. He was too far gone: there was no room in his heart for anyone but Suleika. One morning, very early, they ran away to the Kasbah of Tangiers, where the desperate go to hide. They got married. The only way they could do it was if she recited the Shahada: La ilaha illa Allah, Mohammadu rasoul Allah. Eleven words. If it meant they'd be together, she'd have said anything. They moved into a beat-up old shack, but they were happy. They were together. He played his music at a nearby club, and when he finished work, he came home to her.

"After a month, he was on his way home from the club when two men jumped him. The brothers of the girl he'd jilted. Suleika was at home, waiting for him. She knew something was wrong when he didn't show up. At dawn she went to look for him. She found him on the ground, oud smashed at his side. She threw herself on him, covered his body with hers. She howled. An animal in pain. People came running. She clung to him, but they pulled her away. She realized she was completely alone. She didn't know what to do, where to go. She wanted to die with Taleb, to go with him wherever he went. She stood alone all that day, waiting for a sign from him. After a long time she heard a low hum. Taleb's hum. It came from far away, and it drew her. It led her back to her family's sla in the Fuente Nueve. All the Jews were there, praying. When they saw her, most of them threw stones at her. They called her a whore and a traitor. Her mother threw the most stones. 'I've come home,' she told the Jews. But the Arabs from the Kasbah had followed her. 'No way,' they said. 'You're ours now.' A fight broke out. They nearly tore her in half. In the end, the Arabs took her. Because she tried to go back to being a Jew, they killed her."

"I've heard the hum. Outside my window. At first I thought it was Mom. But maybe it's Taleb. Or even Suleika. What could she want from me?"

"It takes more than one life to make a human being," says Papy. "Maybe she's calling you to do something–she didn't have time for."

"Do you believe that story?" I ask him. "That she fell in love with an Arab boy?"

"I have a vision of Suleika as a child. She leans from the roof and watches her father come home. He wears black and

122

goes barefoot–as all Jews did by law in those days. She tries to pick him out but he's indistinguishable from the other Jews. When he enters the house, she doesn't rush down to greet him. She knows he needs to prepare himself first. The first thing he does when he gets home is to change from the black djellabah into a white one–like mine–white as the dream of light. That's where she first understands the nature of light, how it emerges only from the dark. Good from evil, as the Kabbalists used to say. The Jewish women blame her for going where she didn't belong. How else would she have understood? How else would she have returned, the way all voyagers into the soul return, with the memory of the light in their eyes? A neighbor, an Arab boy, the Sultan–all metaphors for the journey she took into a country that has no name."

"But how could she? Choose death, I mean? Dead letters and words, an abstract god, over the taste of an orange, or the feel of rain on her face?"

"Brita, the Hebrew letters are a form of God. *Shin*: proud, sullen pitchfork. *Lamed*: loose and graceful as a clear wave in the sea. *Aleph*: who can't make up his mind and wants to have it all ways at once–arms and legs moving left and right, up and down. Once you begin, you can get lost. Everything in the universe is alive, including letters. And the letters of His Name are rich and pulsing with life. That's why we can't speak them but can only call him ha' Shem, or The Name."

"Was He there, waiting for her on the other side of the

door? Waiting with open arms? Oh, Suleika baby, here I am, the Big Name, waiting for you. Come on in."

"Ask her."

I follow Gaby downstairs to the hushed dark landing. Twenty-two steps between you and me. I touch his shoulder. "I would still rather bite into an orange than into a name."

He turns and looks at me as if he's bitten into something sour. "Brit. I can't breathe in your story."

"Maybe I can't breathe in yours either."

"You're not in my story. Got it?"

I gulp in the heavy, dark air, but he's gone before I can answer. I go to my room and close the door, move to the window and stare at the mimosa tree as if I am on the Exodus, staring at the vision of light in the desert. As if Papy is right: no time has passed. I'm still eleven years old, staring at Kunkle's Furniture Store window on Liberty Bell Road in Horsens. What Old Man Kunkle had set up: a tribute to the American Family Christmas, 1962. In the first window, the couch and chair were Early American, solid oak. An artificial fire blazed in the fireplace. Two smiling blond mannequin children sat in front of a Christmas tree weighted with gold balls, silver bells and wreaths of tinsel. A star flashed on and off at the top of the tree. I wanted that tree. It was mine! The whole room was mine! The gifts scattered on the floor were mine! The fire was supposed to warm *me*, the light cast its soft shadow on *me*.

I moved to the next window, looked in the kitchen, and saw the mother. Blonde, blue-eyed as her children, she smil-

ingly reached to pull something from the oven. A pie? Pump-
kin or mince? Plum pudding? Almost close enough to touch,
in her blue and white gingham apron.

In the next window, the father, brown-haired, blue-eyed,
sat on the bed, leaning forward to put on his brown leather
slippers. One foot in a gray sock lightly touched the hard-
wood floor. The other foot was already half in the slipper. He
looked tired, but a healthy tired—weary from a day's work at
the office. No remote, faraway look in his blue eyes. This father couldn't wait to join the children in the living room,
was already tasting his wife's pie.

I glared at the people standing outside, next to me. A
family—father, mother, two children—like the family in the
windows. The kids were so heavily bundled I couldn't see
their faces. The father wore transparent, horn-rimmed
glasses, not like Dad's dark glasses which were designed to
make sure no one saw his eyes. The mother had shiny pale
brown hair. They smiled at the windows, smiled in recogni-
tion. "Isn't that sweet?" said the mother. The father put his
arm around her. "Next year we'll get a four-poster," he said,
"just like that one."

They spoke fearlessly, distinctly, their English pure and
true. I heard Mom clicking her teeth as she struggled over
absurd words—hippopotamus, anniversary, spaghetti—until
she turned red with frustration. And Dad, slurring the final
syllables of every word, the endings of sentences in his rush
to disguise his accent.

These mothers didn't have a gold tooth like Mom's. The

mother next to me didn't have hair that fell in a tangle of black curls to her waist. Her hair was tight and controlled, a gleaming silk cap. The mother in the window didn't cook couscous and dafina, or use spices like cumin, za'atar or ksboor. The father never saw her seeking her future in spread-out mint tea leaves, or dancing on bare, round feet to Enrico Macias and Jo Amar. No! This mother and father danced decorously to "sleighbells ring–are you listening? . . . " wafting from the store's loudspeaker. I could almost smell their world: the pie baking, the fresh evergreen tree, the piney, woodsy scent.

I went inside the main entrance of the store and pushed past the smiling salesmen until I came to the display window with the children and the tree. From within the store, it was different. I saw the wires and lights flashing. The children looked plastic and unreal–their faces too evenly pink, their mouths tiny painted red hearts, their eyes empty blue glass. Even the tree was only decorated in front, its sharp green needles flattened and empty from the back.

I entered the cozy living room of the window. It was very hot: the lights, glowing wires and heat made my head swim. I took another step in, and another, careful not to trip over the wires and cords in my red galoshes (two sizes too big). Where to station myself? What was my role? I smiled down at the little boy opening an electric train set and the girl clutching a doll as fair and uniformly pink as she was. I willed myself to appear innocent, pure: a Christian from Paris. Who could imagine that inside this jacket and dress, the neatly braided hair, hid a Jew? I pretended to know nothing of djnoun, martyred Jews, ghosts and spirits. I belonged here. "I'm your cousin from Paris," I said softly. "Don't you recognize me?"

They didn't respond, so I turned to my audience. My audience! A surprise visit to Horsens, Pennsylvania, from the one and only Brit Lek, here on loan from the Royal Marrakesh–I mean, the Royal Paris Theater. Let's give her a hand and welcome her!

The people outside the window were dim and blurred in the fog. I saw overcoats, shadowed features, indistinct movements, a large pointed finger. So that's how it is from in here. We're warm, protected, golden. And you all look the same: dark, huddled, faceless. Maybe that was how it was meant to be: always an inside, always an outside. Someone has to be in, and someone has to be out. We can't all be inside. I needed to tell Dad: we can't all squeeze into this small room.

I FALL ASLEEP IN MY CLOTHES, on Mom's blue and red velvet tapestry, and wake up around noon. A folded piece of paper lies on the floor, near the door. I open it and read: *There's someone I want you to meet. This afternoon? We'll bring Christian from Paris reinforcements: Sylvie and Luc.*

WE START OUT SCRUPULOUSLY POLITE, BUT MOCKING: Niece and Tonton. Since I asked Mani to invite Luc (whom I have only danced with a couple of times), I insist he accompany us, too.

Gaby's pale yellow Citroën looks like a Volkswagon Bug, parked on the rue Moulay-Youssef outside the mellah. Boys wipe the car with rags, sit on the fenders. Gaby gives them coins, and we climb inside. Sylvie sits in front next to Gaby. I get in back, squeezed between Mani and Luc.

"The sky is gray," says Mani, craning his head out the window as we drive down the rue Moulay-Youssef. "Is it supposed to rain today?"

Luc shrugs. "The radio said there was a small chance of rain."

"I love this air," I say. "Rain without rain." I wish I wasn't in the middle, that I could lean out and feel the air clinging to my cheeks.

Luc smiles at me. About twenty-one, he's lanky like Mani, but broader and more muscular. His passion is soccer. He plays at least once a day, the rest of his time spent working with his father at the Mairie, or dancing at the Majestic. He has the same schoolboy-red cheeks as Tonton Elie (the wild ocean air?) and heavy-lidded hazel eyes that smolder on the strobe-lit dance floor but merely sleep through the gray light of day. He smells good (Eau Sauvage, Sylvie instantly pointed out, when he entered the car), has wavy chestnut hair cut short, an easy smile. I like him. Very much. When he puts his arm around me, I feel the approval of everyone in the car. Even the seat seems to sigh in relief as I let myself lean against his arm. Gaby winks at me in the rearview mirror, and I smile. Okay Tonton, we'll be friends. That's how it will be. I'm tired of fighting. I'm getting myself back on track. Brit

Suleika Lek. American. Free. The girl no one can hold. Another few days, and I'll sling my backpack over my shoulder and head for Fez, pay my respects to Suleika, and fly back to the States.

On the highway outside El Kajda, Gaby picks up speed, and my hair flies around my face and throat. I lean my head forward, and Luc gathers my hair in his hands and winds it into a sort of bun, which he holds firm with his palm at the back of my neck.

"You should put it up." Sylvie pats her own smooth, pale blonde French twist.

"It's the color of leaves," Luc says. "Autumn leaves in Paris."

"More like burnt wood, under the sun," says Gaby. "The kind we use to fire the kiln." His voice is cool, an artist observing colors.

As Gaby turns a sharp curve, Luc lets go and my hair whips my face and tangles around my throat again. "I should cut it, but my mother loved it long."

Mani says, "Turn your head. I'll braid it." His hands separate my hair into three strands, then twine them into a long, thick braid. Sylvie hands him a rubber band, and he winds it around the bottom of the braid. "Watch your own hair," I whisper to Mani as the coarse wig begins its usual slide down the side of his head.

I lean back against Luc's shoulder and look out the side window. Tall slender palm trees line the road along the beach. The waves crash a few feet away from us. A light-

house with turrets rises like a castle in a fairy tale. Fishermen sell their catch by the side of the road, and boys hold
out seashell necklaces. We fly past a faded blue bus, a man
mounted on the roof, slipping back and forth as he straps on
the passengers' luggage.

Gaby drives like a demon, skimming the road. Sylvie
clings with both hands to the dashboard, obviously terrified
but silent. Luc looks green and Mani simply resigned, holding his wig with one hand, while I slide back and forth between them. "Tonton!" His eyes are dark, unreadable in the
rearview mirror. "Slow down!"

He immediately slows to a crawl. "We're here anyway."

"Where?" Luc asks.

"Azemmour. I hope Saadia is still alive."

"Who is this guy anyway?" asks Mani.

"I met him years ago, when I went on the ship." Gaby
turns to me. "I want you to hear his story."

As soon as we get out of the car, sea wind blows at us.
Mani has one hand flat on top of his wig. "My hair!" shrieks
Sylvie, both hands gripping her head as if it will fly off. "It's
going to be such a mess!"

"There's a great café in town, at the square," says Gaby.
"For those of you who can still stand to eat fish. The guy I
want to visit lives in the mellah, over there, through the Kasbah."

"Do we have to go, chéri?" asks Sylvie. "How about if we
meet you at the café?"

## the rider and the sea

"Fine," Gaby says. "We won't be long."

Mani joins Sylvie and promises to meet us later.

Salt wind blows Gaby, Luc and me inside the old Kasbah to the mellah, another cramped, claustrophobic space marked off for Jews. Peeling doors without names or numbers, an alley I can span with outstretched arms. Stone steps to one side, an arched tunnel to the other. Weathered yellow houses that look deserted. Few people, and none under sixty. A fat, kerchiefed woman, knife and potato in her hands, watches us with milk-flecked brown eyes. We pass a tiny, empty café, a literal hole in a wall, with two small round tables. An open doorway to our right frames two old men seated at a table, clutching each other's bald heads.

Around a sharp corner, we bump into a tiny sparrow of a woman. Shrieking "ah'wili aa'lina!" she pulls at tufts of hennaed orange hair and scratches her cheeks, drawing blood. The air is dingy, sour with the smell of piss, shit, garbage piled on the street. Human decay, hopelessness—but muted, numbed—like the people's eyes, gestures, cries, as if they have suffered so long the pain has become part of daily life. Unable to go one step farther, I grip my throat and lean against an abandoned fruit stall, flies drinking from bursting purple-black figs.

Luc bends over me. "Are you okay?"

"It's too much. I can't."

"I don't blame you. This place is a death-pit. I wouldn't want to eat at a café here."

131

Gaby grabs my chin and forces my head up. "What's your problem? Who do you think you are? A tourist?" The mask of politeness is gone, the eyes furious again.

Luc watches us, hands in his pockets. Gaby is right: Luc is the tourist here. Not me. Otherwise this place wouldn't grab my heart so powerfully and hurt so deeply. But why is he still so angry at me? Last night was a turning point for me. I have no fear left. "Tell me the truth. Why are you always so mad at me? And pretending you're not?" He begins to protest, but I talk over his words. "Don't deny it please. It can't be just because of the spell. What is it?"

"Nothing. Now are you afraid to get your feet dirty? Or are you coming with me?"

I follow him silently, Luc on my heels.

Saadia Ohana is a grizzled fisherman with immense hairy nostrils, one crushed leg beneath him, a small pointed head. His right eye is filmy, clouded. He looks like a huge primeval insect, but he has a wonderful deep laugh, from the gut. He is well over a hundred years old, possibly even one hundred twenty years old. No one, including Saadia himself, knows for sure, because when he was born they did not keep records.

The small room is filthy. No chairs. A striped mattress in the corner on which Saadia sits. Two cracked cups on a small table with curving legs. Tin utensils on the brown sink. I don't blame Luc for withdrawing nearly to the door in an effort to escape the piss-sharp stink of sickness, dirt, rotting food. Gaby sits on the floor near the mattress, laughing and talking in Arabic with the old man. I understand one word in ten. He turns in mid-laugh and says, "Saadia used to fish from his second story window. He'd reel in the line, and the fish flopped on his bedroom floor."

I'm barely listening, intrigued by the glimpse of a gold tooth in Gaby's mouth, far back, upper right. His teeth are white and square, and then that one gold tooth. Like Mama Ledicia's, like my mother's.

"Listen to this, Brit. He knew the Hatchuels–Suleika's family–actually knew them when he lived in Rabat."

"But how could he? Wasn't it ages ago?"

"She died in the 1800s. He knew her brother. I'm going to ask him to tell you what he remembers."

I sit on the floor, but as Saadia talks and Gaby keeps turning to translate his Arabic into French, I lean forward and move closer and closer until Gaby pushes me in front of him. While he translates–whispering over my shoulder, in my ear–he starts playing with my hair. At first I can't believe it's him. I turn around fast, he looks slightly dazed and drops his hand. I turn back to face Saadia, and slowly, lightly, his hand returns. He pulls off the rubber band and whispers, "Let me fix your hair, okay?" I nod, and he combs through the long windblown curls with his fingers. Even though his hands are gentle, there's no way to go through it without a brush. He hits a clump of hair, and I wince. "Sorry," he says. His hand rests on the back of my head as he talks to me. I want to cry suddenly, thinking of what I've lost: a real uncle, not like Elie or Haim, who are both useless to me, but someone who is unshockable, who knows everything about the dance between men and women, an artist who can teach me so much. Maybe it's not too late. Maybe we can be friends the way we used to be. I sit back and listen to Saadia's deep, slow voice and Gaby's words in my ears.

"Haim Hatchuel was my friend. The famous Isso Hatchuel's son. People were scared of the Hatchuels. A cursed family. First, there was Suleika. The virgin martyr who gave her life to God. Then her older brother, Isso, who went broke and mad, trying to save his sister. But poor Haim. A failure. A man who tried everything and succeeded at nothing. Everyone loved him. Even the Arabs swore he was a man of honor. A good man. Kind and loving to his family and friends. He married and had kids. But no matter what he tried, he didn't have the money touch. He smelled of failure. The family was in ruins. Old Isso, deaf and senile. The children reduced to beggars. Or running barefoot in rags, like savages. Even though Haim was older than I was, I tried to help him by offering him work in my father's restaurant. My father, my uncle and I ran a café by the river, near the mellah entrance, on the rue Oukasa. We had our own gate in the Andalusian wall, opposite the Place du Mellah. To enter our café, you had to bend over to enter through a huge circle opening. The café was white and blue. You drank tea and ate over the waters of the Bou-Regreg. Nothing could be all bad when you watched the river roll past. And the life of it! Children swimming, women washing clothes, people gathering to gossip. The people of Salé waving to us from the other side of the river. We were still so many then. We had seventeen synagogues!

"Haim brought his father, Old Isso, to the café. Old Isso looked like one of the patriarchs. White hair flowed down his back. He had a long white beard. He carried a cane. And he shouted when he spoke. Deaf in one ear. I used to think he was blind, too. He didn't see us. He looked straight at me, I remember, and I swear he had no idea I stood in front of him. You could see he'd been a handsome man. Haim was, too. Well, the whole family had a strange beauty. I fell in love with his younger sister. T'bark'Allah, the most beautiful girl I have ever seen in my life. Eyes–hair–body–I can't describe her in words. Language can't touch her beauty. And me, I was never handsome–always short and ugly. Normally, I'd never have gone near a beauty like that. But there was something in her face, a light in her eyes that dared me. And I was still a boy, no older than eighteen. I went to her. I didn't tell Haim. I knew he'd pity me for being a fool. She didn't laugh at me. I was sure she would, but she didn't. She listened to what I had to say. And because she listened so intently, almost snatching the words–still unspoken–from my mouth, I went on and said more than I'd intended. I bared myself to her. I looked in her eyes and gave her my love, asked her to marry me, begged her to give me a chance. When I ran out of things to offer, I stopped and knew, by her eyes, that it could never be. She was a star, fallen to earth. This wasn't her true home. She didn't belong here on the ground with us. She said to me, 'I am going to do the kindest thing I've ever done in my life,

Saadia Ohana. I am going to set you free. You are a good man, and you don't deserve me.' She left me at the opening to my café and disappeared into the mellah.

"The next thing I heard was that she ran away with David Abitbol. He had bad blood and was as poor as her family, but he was tall and handsome. Haim hated him, and so did I. He didn't walk: he crept. You never heard him approach. A snake of a man. But so good-looking that the girls of good family did anything to get his attention. After she left with him, I couldn't bear Rabat anymore. Even Haim could talk of nothing but his problems. When I think back at how we avoided him and his family, I am ashamed. How when he brought Old Isso to the café, everyone moved away. As if the sight of them hurt. No one helped them. We watched them suffer, starve, die. I gave up on Haim when I saw he couldn't make it in the café either. Two of his sisters had tuberculosis. They came back home to live after their husbands died. Each one had a couple of kids. Everyone crowded in a shack, sleeping on the floor, no food, no hope. Old Isso, deaf and blind, waving his cane and shouting about Suleika to anyone who would listen. Haim, scrambling on the street for a dirham, a centime, to feed his clan. And most of Rabat avoiding them as if they had the plague. It's over now.

"Those days are gone. I pray they're at peace, and that they forgive us. Did we know then that Suleika died for us? Did we know about the massacres yet to come? We knew nothing. We still know nothing. And my Sol must be laughing somewhere. She thought that she had set me free. Look at me, more than a half-century later. Alone as the day I was born, crippled, penniless, childless. All the young ones left years ago. I don't think anyone even remembers us, the few who are left. I can count us on two hands. Too poor to leave, too stubborn and old. Where would we go? It's over now. I have nothing left but my memories."

Outside Saadia's room, the rain is so thick it floods the cobbled street. Scraps of paper whirl past, fruit rinds, torn cardboard, a black shoe. I see my grandmother Alice running through another mellah, past rivers of human bones. Luc looks miserable. I wish I'd never asked Mani to bring him. Gaby is behind me, striking one match after another, but the wet wind extinguishes them. I turn and cup my hands around his to help him. He strikes another match and lowers his head to catch the flame with the end of his cigarette. He blows out the flame and straightens up, cigarette lit and clenched in the corner of his mouth.

My hands are still tented around his. His hands are larger and darker, ridged and bumpy, but we have the same slender fingers, rounded knuckles, narrow wrists. I'm sure that if I turn his hand over and look behind the gathered, bleached skin of his palm, I'll see a familiar map of tiny crisscrossing lines. Blood-intimacy. A knowledge that speaks behind words, without sound, in dream-images. The pigeons fly past, painted brilliant and harsh streaks. Their wings flutter between us. An old man winds a rose slowly and gently around a little girl's ear. A big boy pushes the little girl onto his lap and rests his chin on her head.

*Such was the end of the beautiful and sad Sol Hatchuel.* The Jews of Morocco, in the midst of the pain and suffering that have followed them ceaselessly, retain only a vague memory of the heroic young girl. Now and then, in the Jewish quarter of Tangiers, you're lucky if you hear the women singing a qerida to Suleika.

Sol's parents have been dead a long time. Her brother Issachar died in 1868, leaving a widow with five daughters and a son. The family lives in the direst misery.

I thought that more than one reader of this paper would be happy to give, in memory of doña Sol, a charitable donation to the members of her family. Not only would this financial support help to alleviate their abject misery, but it would demonstrate to the family's descendants that courageous Sol and her honorable brother are not completely forgotten.

Please send donations to M. Le Directeur of the Archives Israëlites. I promise to transfer them immediately to these poor people.

—Isidore Loeb,
*Archives Israëlites,*
1880

## *strange and tender beast*

"I DON'T KNOW WHERE YOUR HEART IS," she said, staring at our hands in the rain while I looked at her. In my throat, I almost said, but my heart beat in my throat and I couldn't form words. "In your hands I think," she said, as I pulled them away. "They show what you can't."

CAN EVERYTHING CHANGE IN A DAY? It started with her hair. Or the smell of her. Or even earlier, on the roof? This is my home, the pôterie hill. The ground can't shift beneath me here. My brother, my brother, watch over me. My sister, help me be strong.

IN THE CAR ON THE WAY BACK TO EL KAJDA, everyone talked at once, the day having turned into a surprising success. Excited, she leaned forward to tell me her thoughts about wild Sol and Saadia's story: "I'm beginning to see that Suleika was real. Not just Mom's lesson to me, or a legend. She was a real girl, flawed and breathing, a girl who got her period and who cried and laughed and fell in love with the wrong guy too, and left a brother and sad family behind. And then

139

was forgotten by everyone. Was it worth it, Gaby? Who did Suleika die for exactly? That's what I still don't understand."

I wondered what she'd say if she knew I had made up at least half of the story. Unable to concentrate. Searching for something. Eyes fixed on the long, tangled mass of hair falling down her back as we sat in Saadia's room. I needed to use my hands, to touch. She lifted her hair with both hands and bared her nape. Her head fell forward as if she were Suleika on the block. I wanted to pull her back to safety. I reached for her hair. When she trembled and looked back at me, I said with my hands: you're so young, it's not over yet, just let me touch your hair. My fingers brushed against her nape. Curved like a wave. I pushed my fingers through her hair from underneath so I was caught in the wildfire tangle. What are you doing? my sister asked me. Why are your hands in my daughter's hair? It's nothing, I said. Meaningless. I'm just going to braid her hair. I need to do something with my hands, Sheba.

I tried to comb through the mass with my fingers, to spread out the crackling sea before me. Orange-blue sparks lit and darted, fireflies. I reached a small nest of matted hair. Couldn't get through it.

"It hurts!"

Shhh, it's all right, I said with my hands again, abandoning the fight, approaching my true mission: to braid her hair. There was something in the weaving, twining motion I needed. I felt as if I worked the clay. Winding thick coils, setting one over the other, and the third one over that. Tightening the braid, interlocking. Leaving no room for air to escape. I finished quickly, wound the rubber band, and dropped my hands. Kept on telling her the story, taking a phrase from Saadia and winding it to an image of mine, braiding the words around her. Rain beat on the roof, entered through the cracks in the ceiling, and the openings in her hair no matter how hard I had tried to seal them. The walls fell open, and we were in the jungle. I smelled something raw and ancient, but sweet, like a baby. Rainwater and cinnamon. I leaned closer, whispered the story in her ear, tracing the curve of cheek to chin to throat with my voice. A large bird swooped low, almost touched my shoulder, then flew off again toward the wild beating trees. Is it you? Are you calling me, little cat?

As I drove through the Bab Sha'aba, just at the entrance of El Kajda, a mokhazni on his motorcycle signaled for me to pull over. Merde, I thought, not now. When all I can focus on is the braiding motion, fingers moving in and out–I can't lose it, something I need to grasp–

I got out of the car. It was Farid, Salim's brother, who had just joined the force. I'd seen him at the port a few times. "You were speeding," he began.

"No, I wasn't."

He glowered. "Your car is too full. How many people do you have in there? You know the law–"

"I'm in a hurry. How much?"

"Are you bribing me?"

I slipped him fifteen dirhams. Salim used to be happy with ten, but I didn't like Farid's squinty eyes. And every delay hurt.

I returned to pandemonium in the car. I didn't get it at first. I started the car and drove into town. Mani was explaining to Sylvie and Brit, who couldn't understand. "I told you," said Mani, "he recognized Gaby's car. He knows he's a Jew. All Gaby has to do is pay a fine, and everything is okay."

"That's right," I said. But Sylvie was furious, her voice a shriek. "Pay a fine for what? For being a Jew? I told you we should move to Paris!"

"It's degrading! Dehumanizing!" cried Brit, leaning forward.

"For him too," I said. "For fifteen dirhams, he becomes a uniform without a face."

"Yes, but he doesn't have to pay a fine for—just for existing," said Brit.

While they argued, I drove through town around the Place de France—French, Europeans, rich Jews and Arabs sitting at cafés and restaurants. Turned left at the Drb el B'har past the warehouses to the Place Q'dma—and the Café Chez Toufik, maybe the only completely integrated place in the whole town, where whores, hustlers and drug dealers of all religions and races smoke water pipes, drink coffee and Pernod, and work the black market. While I drove to the beach beyond the Majestic, images filled my head. Without sequence or logic. The absence of light and color, of meaning. No Arabs dancing at the Majestic. No Jews in the medina. The key was in Farid and me. I still couldn't grasp it, but I felt the borders cracking and tearing, seeping through like the rain in Saadia's room, Arabs and Jews working together at the port, all the Arab businesses with Jewish names—the result of forced conversions through the centuries. What were these people, a few generations down the line, what are they? Jews or Arabs, or a mixture of both: Arabs with Jewish memory? What are we but Arab Jews? In Paris I never felt at home with the European Jews. I was more comfortable with the pieds noirs, all of us with our black African hearts and feet.

I parked near the club, on the deserted stretch of sand that extended to the Portuguese fortress. The rain had stopped. We took off our shoes and walked barefoot along the beach, thick gold sand crumbling between our toes. Sky and waves blurred in a vast black-gray mist. Vapor rose like steam from the foam. I felt strange in my skin, the flesh of my hands contracting and pinching, like too-tight shoes. I had a headache and wished I could be alone.

Luc bent over and wrote in the sand with a stick. Sylvie read aloud, as he wrote: "'Luc and Brit.' How sweet. A shame it's going to wash away."

I flexed my hands, trying to make the flesh fit the bone again. My hands contracted whenever it rained or I was near moisture. I stretched my fingers as far as they could go. I went out with a pianist once. At night and in the morning, she stretched her fingers until they reminded me of crawling centipedes.

"Nothing's ever lost," said Brit. "It will just resurface somewhere else. Don't you think?"

No one answered, but Luc beamed at her. I was getting sick of his smug red face. Getting sick of everyone. Sylvie hanging onto my arm—because she refused to take off her high heels and they kept sinking in the sand. Mani bowing low to Brit: "Want to practice our routine now?"

They danced on the sand to silence, two thin awkward figures suddenly graceful. Mani slithering and sliding around her, over her, crouching to a split and effortlessly rising. His moves were smoother and sweeter, hers more brutal and thrusting. They danced, hip to hip. Poor kid, with his wig slipping off. I think if it were me, I'd take it off altogether and force people to get used to me as I am. If I'm hairless, so be it.

She pulled off the rubber band, ran her hands through the hair, and let it tumble over her shoulders and down her back. Even in the dark, her hair glowed with flames and midnight-blue shadows. Her bracelets rang like small bells as she whirled. My hands stopped flexing and groped the air. It was a movement I searched for. The key. Her hair brushed my arm as she swung around. How could I have thought she was a little girl? Maybe I tried to keep my little cat stopped in time, like a photo—one thing pure and unchanged at least. But she was a woman. The way she moved, sliding her hips around Mani's. The way she had the soccer player unable to take his eyes off her. It was more than beauty: you watched her face to see what she would do next.

Her hair again. A teasing touch—light and glancing—but it

made the hair on my arm prickle. I remembered when I bit her hair. She had told me a story about India while we sat on the curb of that godforsaken place in America she called home, facing one of the red-brick monstrosities that lined the street. The sky was dulled gray, tired. People's eyes dead and flat, as if they'd been pressed into books. Even Sheba with her glorious liquid black eyes was deadened, the spark extinguished. While Joseph had no eyes at all. Black glasses he wore even at the dinner table at night. The light hurts his eyes, explained Sheba. The light? Or the sight of us: reminders of who you are, Lek, you cold bastard? I'm a Christian from Paris, she told me, and I wanted to shake her hard, hard—and say, you fucking little fool, I held you a minute after you were born, even before your father. I took you to the window and we looked into the courtyard together, and I swear we saw the same thing, just for a second, as if we looked through one pair of eyes. I was only thirteen or fourteen, but when you learned to walk, I was the one you walked to: arms stretched out in front of you, wavering side to side, laughing as if you'd given me the greatest gift. And you had. "She trusts you," my mother said. "She sees Gaby," Sheba said, smiling.

I don't know why you made me so angry with your Christian-from-Paris story. But I bought candies from a dead-faced old man, and we sat and ate them—and I wanted to shut out the rage, so I said, "I heard that you want to be a writer. Tell me a story."

You didn't play coy or shy. You said, "I'm going to make it

145

up as I go along. Are you afraid of camels?" When I shook my head, you said, "Good. Then we'll go to the camel festival in–in Rajistan. We'll ride through the desert . . . to a walled fortress town named . . . named Pushkar. It rises out of the desert like a dream. The men have long black handlebar mustaches and gentle black eyes. They wear magenta turbans. The women are flowers. They dance as they move. We'll stay at the zanana, the old harem, on the second floor. We can look out of the brown lattice windows. No one can see us, but we see everything that's happening on the main street. There's a full moon, no wind. The street is starting to fill up for the festival. We see lepers on the side of the road. Bearded sadus in their loincloths. Hindus praying. Rajputs– camel nomads who travel from town to town all year long. And harem women singing desert songs about their men– they call them their strange and tender beasts. The women's voices are haunting, so passionate and wild that we peek out farther to see them. We can almost see their breasts, their bare brown midriffs. But their hair and faces are covered. They hold their veils between their teeth."

"Like this." I lifted a thick coil of your hair, clenched it between my teeth and bit it. I felt I had entered your story, that I was the Terror of India stalking a strange and tender beast.

"The . . . the men set up booths and tents for the camel festival. Traders lead strings of Arabian horses with small hooves and their ears turned in."

I lifted my hands and pressed my ears against my head, your hair still caught between my teeth.

146

"They make us feel small. The moon, the desert, the travelers from everywhere. All the strangers. They make us wonder—who we are."

She stopped on the sand in front of me, laughing—the way no other woman laughs here. Moroccan women know better, the invitation it suggests, the possible danger. My sisters learned early: never meet a man's eyes, never smile openly at a man. But she doesn't smile, she laughs instantly, her whole face a sudden sun explosion. "Tonton, want to dance?"

"Without music?"

Sylvie frowned, tightened her grip on my arm. Mani started singing one of his American soul songs.

"Mani taught me that we become the music when we dance."

I couldn't compete with Mani. No one could. I didn't want to dance with this sweaty, laughing tigress. Sheba's girl. My hands reached for her. Something I was groping for. That I'd forgotten. Where was it? What was it?

"Slow dance, Tonton?"

She sounded surprised. I mumbled that I couldn't dance fast without music. She seemed disappointed, stood back from me. I pressed one hand at the back of her neck, and the other against the flat of her back—through the damp curling hair. I was too close. How had I gotten this close to my niece? Her hair still smelled of cinnamon and rain, so sweet and raw it made me dizzy. If I bite into your hair now, little girl, what will you do? You don't know what you're asking for.

Don't press your wet cheek against mine. Don't breathe so fast it's like a tiny heart fluttering against my throat. The waves reached our feet, swirled around our ankles. I loved the feel of having my feet wet as I danced with her. I gripped a thick coil of her hair with one hand, mashed it against her back with my palm.

"I could only believe in a god who could dance," she said against the side of my throat.

I didn't say anything, grabbed the hair harder. Her face was too close, her forehead, her lashes.

"Nietzsche said that. I believe it. Do you?"

"Yes."

"You're not listening."

"I am."

She moved back. I forced myself to return to the sand, the eyes on us. "Thank you for taking me to Saadia." Eyes enormous, darker than the waves. Sheba's eyes. But not restful like Sheba's. Probing. What did she want now?

Luc stood by me, trying to look respectful. I felt old suddenly. I was old. Nearly thirty. Too old to play these games. I pulled away. "Your girl," I told him and backed off. Lit a cigarette and looked at the waves.

The sea was shrinking. Didn't anyone else see how it was closing in on us? Contracting, like the flesh on my hand. The waves curling in, question marks that turned into hooks, hooks that should slide over the wet sand but that gutted it like a fish eye. The sea was rancid, stank of everyone's garbage, plastic bags ripped open, labels and wrappers, trash strewn and floating. It stank of death, the hook-waves clawed the sand. The horizon was almost on us, moving in behind the waves, lurking in the shadow of the hooks, a great black grin. I could just see the points of its teeth biting the sky.

It was time to go. I had to get out of here. I couldn't remember feeling this depressed in a long time. I turned around and saw Sylvie watching me. How was I going to slip out of this one? The noose already tightening around my neck. Brit, Luc and Mani were moving toward the club. "Go with them," I told Sylvie. "I'll be there in a minute."

She pouted, but went off, holding onto Mani's arm. Watching her wiggle away, I wondered what I'd ever seen in her. Dancing with Brit had reminded me what was missing in my life: passion. Time for a new one. Time to move on. I just wished I wasn't so tired, so fucking weary of the whole cycle. There had to be something more.

As soon as they left me alone on the sand, my heart began to lighten. I remembered the motion I'd been groping for all day. Farid and me. A wall between us. Taleb seeing Suleika through a hole in the wall. A painting in which colors and forms bled into each other. I shaped the wall with my hands. The gap in the center, a hole you peek through, like barbed wire. And then I saw it. The braiding motion. Strand over strand. Twisting and turning moist, malleable flesh into what is rigid, harsh, electrified.

I was out of there and at the pôterie in fifteen minutes. Only Ibrahim was there. "I thought you'd come tonight. Look at the moon."

Blood-red and diffused, with dots of light that extended like rays of sun. I hadn't looked up all night, my eyes focused on the movement of waves in a woman's hair.

"Mohammed is up there, watching us."

"Or Moses."

He laughed and slapped me on the back. "Brothers. Like you and me."

"Brothers."

The rest was a blur. Lighting the oil lamps in the shed, drawing out my clay from the large bag, getting my tools together, until I finally wedged the clay, fingers digging and clawing deep inside, choking off every secret pocket of air, every bubble and opening. When the clay was ready for me, I let go of the memories stored inside: her hair, flames and cinnamon, her color dark-red like the blood moon, like fire, her bleeding heart. And the twisting, twining braids. I wound three long coils of clay, stared at them, and closed my eyes. A man in green and a man in black stared at each other across a barbed wire fence. Enemies, though they could no longer remember why. Each man held a machine gun aimed at the other. The sky was vast, pale. Around them was desolation, dead burnt ground, the sound of rockets exploding. The war zone. As I moved closer, I saw the fence was electrified. With every breath of air, the wire emitted sparks. The border between you and me. The no-man's-land no one can survive. Barbed wire separates us. The man in green lowers his machine gun and stares at the man in black. He lets the gun fall to the ground. The other man remains tense, motionless, gun aimed at the enemy. The unarmed man takes a step toward the barbed wire. Another step. The other man cocks his gun and aims.

I opened my eyes. Sweat dripped down my forehead into my eyes. My hands were already struggling to get through, my fingers clawing between the tangled wires. I twisted the wire until the holes were too small to reach through. But maybe an eye could see through. Taleb's eye seeing Suleika through the hole in the wall. Brit glimpsing me through a keyhole. It all came together. Borders cracking, each side seeping into the other. Farid lost his name, became only a uniform. While I became the Jew with the yellow car to him. Yellow car, yellow star. Eye like a star peered through. My fingers ached as I wove the clay, until it was about sixty centimeters long, thirty centimeters high, and about two centimeters thick. I felt I worked with rusted wire that cut into my heart. You wondered where my heart is, little cat. Here, in the clay. Here, in my throat. My hands.

I SCREAM ON THE HILL, FROM MY LUNGS AND GUTS, arms reaching toward the sky, toward my brother, the bloody moon, whatever your name is. I love you. I love everyone. I've just begun building the wall–the fucking wall! I want to cry and scream and laugh. Ibrahim still snoring away. My brother, the watchman. My sister, somewhere near. You're here, I know you are. I want her, Sheba. I don't know where or how it started, but I want her. It has nothing to do with Sylvie. Or anyone else. She's not the next one. Oh God, I'm drunk. On her, on life. I know it can't go on. One night, Sheba. Would it be so wrong? I swear I won't hurt her. She's mine too, Sheba. And I'll put her on the bus to Fez myself. Just one night, Sheba—out of her whole life.

I hear a gliding sound. Turn and see silver wheels, a bike riding toward me. Mani's bike. I forgot about them at the club. The bike stops. A head leans forward. "Gaby?"

Not you. Not now. I'm scraped raw, too drained and drunk to fight.

She gets off the bike and comes to me, flings her arms around me and leans against my chest. "I was worried about you."

The smell of her—clean, pure, sweet—rises. Some form of sanity clutches in my chest. "Were you? Why?" My voice is as cool as I can make it. It's all I can do not to grab her hair and press her hard against me. My hands hang stupidly at my sides.

She steps back. "Sylvie was mad but I knew you'd be here."

"How?"

"On the beach you were moving your hands, and I knew you must be dying to get back here. What did you work on? Can I see?"

I take her down the stone stairs to the shed and light kerosene lanterns. I follow her eyes as she looks around at the plastic bags of red clay and the shelves filled with bowls and jars in various stages of construction: some still red-

152

brown, soft and wet; others colorless, dried, ready to be glazed. About a dozen finished large plates, candlesticks and tajine bowls painted black and brown and blue against a white background. A few large one-armed vessels overlaid with silver filigree wire standing by the entrance. A tin tub, its edges heaped with bars of speckled soap, brushes, sponges, wet rags.

"It's like the Arabian Nights down here." She stops in front of the long worktable where my barbed wire wall stands. The ends on both sides are unfinished, in tatters, ragged edges forking and drooping in midair. She circles it, bends down, reaches out, then looks at me. "Can I touch?"

"Of course." I move closer until I'm facing her across the wall.

She touches the clay lightly, peering through the small holes. "It's Suleika's wall, isn't it?"

I put my hands over hers. I remember how she looked when she saw the burns for the first time. What else didn't you see with those eyes? I wanted to ask her. Eyes like the sea, but you see nothing.

She's staring at our hands again. With a trembling smile, she looks up at me, leaning toward her across the table, and says, "Can I tell you something?"

Sure you can, bella. Tell me you love me. It will be the perfect opening.

"I realized today how stupid I was being, how I was ruining what could be one of the best relationships in my life. You're—you create—and I want to but I don't know how. And I

153

scared you away. Mom always told me I have no limits or boundaries. If I'd just been a–a normal niece, I know you would have been as gentle and wonderful as you were that day in Horsens. I ruined it, but I wanted you to know that it was partly because I wanted to *be* you–not just love you–but be like you."

"Shut up." My voice is so harsh it shocks even me. I let go of her hands and step back.

She straightens. "I mean it. You're as lonely as I am. I know you are. You know what else Mom used to tell me? That we were two of a kind, you and me. Rebels against nature. I wish I could start over, rewrite this story, and be so much wiser. Then I could learn from you. How to go on with a job you hate, trying to fill the emptiness, but still having the strength to come here by yourself and create something that makes people see what they can't see alone."

I stare at her in the dim yellow light. She is like one of my vessels: the pregnant moon. Dazzling, a vision of light. Like some Joan of Arc fighting for her rights. What was I looking for? What was I trying to do here? Is this a joke, Sheba? Why are you doing this to me? I would have been good to her. I would have made her cry out in joy. I know exactly how I would have touched her. I'd put my arms around her from behind and lift her hair the way she did in Saadia's room. Then I would look at the nape of her neck. Until she felt my eyes burn through the flesh and she shivered. Then I would press my mouth there, in the spot where the wave curls.

"Friends, Tonton?"

"Stop calling me Tonton."

"Sorry, I–" Her skin, luminous like Sheba's, captures every bit of light, hugs it to her. "Maybe you don't want to be friends. I just wanted you to know how I feel. And listen, I won't bother you anymore. I'm going to take a bus to Fez tomorrow."

I'm still staring at her. The mouth now, the upper lip, full like Sheba's, and the lower lip, thin like her father's. She licks her lips. I'm making her nervous.

"I guess in another life–maybe." She licks her lips again. I think she's near tears. I don't want to hurt you, little cat. Just get out of here. Now. "Well, goodnight then." She turns and almost trips over a bucket on the floor, and walks as fast as she can to the stairs, her back rigid, shoulders stiff. Go, please go, as fast as you can. I'm the King of the Underworld down here, evil pouring from my fingertips. I turn my back so I won't be tempted to call her back. The door slams shut behind her.

I take a deep breath. I want to smash something. Why did she have to come here? I've never brought a woman down here before. This is my place. Now I'll always see her here, smell her, feel her hands under mine. Here, in the only place that was mine.

I spray my fucking beautiful wall. Why didn't I carve larger holes through the wire? Why make it impossible to penetrate from one side to the other? Is that what the whole

fucking story comes down to? Two people standing on opposite sides of the wall? Groping in the dark, unable to
reach each other.

I RIDE HOME, A FLEET SWIFT SHADOW IN THE DARK. It's all
downhill, and my hair flies out behind me like a cape. I
won't cry. Not over him. Not ever again. I'm starting to feel
that he exists to make me suffer. I remember Sun God looking down at me after we made love and saying, "No matter
what I do, I feel you are in your own world. I can't reach you.
After all this time, it's as if we're still strangers."

We were strangers. Even Ti, whom I adored and caressed
more lovingly than I ever did Sun God, even with her, I
stayed remote, watching us from a distance, from the peach-
gray walls of her room. I sucked her breasts and ran my
hands down her belly and hips. I loved the cool silk softness
of her skin. I giggled and play-acted with her. I was always
the boy of course. She only wanted to be the girl. I didn't
mind playing the boy. I immediately pretended I was the
Blue Man, my fearless gentle hero. Because he was blue, he
knew what it meant to be different and alone. Because he
was blue, he saw the world the way no one else did. He
charmed everyone, women and men. I thought of him as
something more than male or female, a sort of third gender–
beyond both. The way I was neither Jew nor Christian, but
something else. The Blue Man and I understood each other. I
could become him at a moment's notice. As I rode my bike

down a country road, on my back a knapsack filled with old books: *Lady Chatterly's Lover, The Red and the Black, Villette, Greatheart,* and *The Moonstone,* all bought at an old book barn, none over a quarter, I slid to a stop. An Indian—from India—in a long red and gold brocade gown, maroon fez on his head, stood at the edge of a pale cornfield. A small black dog barked at his side. He smiled and lifted his right hand, palm toward me, in salute, and I knew I had turned into the Blue Man. That night when he entered my dreams, I shared the adventure with him.

Stopping Mani's bike at the mellah gate, I know now why I was so cool with Ti and Sun God. Tonight it was made glaringly obvious that the instant I let go of my emotions I become a blabbering fool, an idiot who doesn't have enough sense to be quiet. What woman in love with a man tells him she yearns to be him? What woman in her right mind—having been rebuffed in every possible way (how could he have been clearer?)—tracks him down yet again, *after* having been told to leave him alone?

When I touched his clay fence tonight and felt his hands pressing over mine, burning with pain, I knew it was hopeless. I'm one of these sad cases who loves once. The tragedy of my life will be that Gaby doesn't love me back. I'm crying again—idiot that I am—as I walk the bike through the mellah gate to the rue du Soleil. I open the green door to my grandparents' house and wheel the bike inside as quietly as I can. Mama Ledicia meets me at the door to my room with a spoonful of honey. "M'shi kapara, na'bibesk." She follows me

157

into my room and sits on the bed with me. "I knew something happened tonight. Believe me, a'b'nti, it's for the best. I am advising you the way I would have advised Sheba, or any of my daughters. If only it weren't Gaby—"

"It's okay, Mamy. I'm leaving tomorrow. Finally I'll go to Suleika, though I still can't see the point."

"Listen to me. Your mother tried everything to have a child. The French doctor in Casablanca told her she was fermée, her pelvis closed. She couldn't have a child. What to do? She couldn't accept his verdict. She went with other women on pilgrimage to the saint, Sidi Rahhal. They spent the night under the tree where he'd patched his djellabah while guarding his flock of sheep. At midnight, the women unwound their long silk sashes and tied them around the tree trunk. They ate leaves from his tree. She waited but nothing happened. Then she went to Suleika. Who would have thought that this girl would become a saint? Did Sheba tell you about her?"

"She told me Suleika was a saint, and that I should try to be like her."

Mama Ledicia shakes her head. "Sheba should have known better. Suleika was a lot more like you than you might think. She was a rebel, one who never listened to her mother, even though her mother tried her best to warn her about the danger outside their door. Suleika didn't listen. She was young, beautiful, and she wanted to go everywhere she pleased.

"One day the next-door neighbor saw her. Ould Lamina

was his name. Fat and middle-aged, he already had a wife, Tahra de Mesmudi. Oh yes, everyone knows their story. Their names are part of our history now. Ould Lamina saw the beautiful young girl and told his wife, 'Get me that girl for a second wife.' Tahra said, 'But she's a Jewess.' Ould Lamina said, 'Get her for me. We'll convert her afterwards.' Tahra was jealous, but she bided her time. After the wedding, when she had the girl in her own courtyard, working for her as the junior wife, then she'd get her revenge.

"Tahra watched the family next door like an eagle. Meanwhile Suleika's mother kept an eye on her daughter, busied her with chores so she couldn't get into mischief. It was Pesach—like now—and you saw how we scour the house top to bottom. Well, Suleika had to do the same. For a week she worked at her mother's side, and the mother finally began to breathe easier. She relaxed her vigilance one afternoon for a moment. That was all it took. Suleika was scrubbing the tiles outside the door. Tahra was outside in a flash. 'My beauty,' she said, 'why does your mother keep you locked away, a flower like you? Come to my house for tea and cakes. Let me brush your hair. If you were my daughter, I'd treat you like a princess. Come to me.' 'My mother won't let me,' said Suleika. 'Why not? Am I evil? A wicked temptress? Come just for a few minutes.' Suleika looked around. Her mother was nowhere in sight. Tahra smiled at her and held out her hand to welcome her into her house. Suleika left her rags and bucket, and followed her. Tahra closed and locked the door behind her.

"Ould Lamina was dancing for joy. But too soon. You see, Suleika was a silly girl, but at heart she was good. She saw this old couple bending over her, insisting she recite the Shahada because the old man was madly in love with her, and she leaped to her feet and tried the door. Locked. She screamed until Ould Lamina tied a cloth around her mouth. Tahra went to the Caid of Tangiers and told him she had a Jewess who had recited the Shahada but who now went back on her word. That's against the law, so the Caid sent guards to Tahra's house. Suleika's mother had found out what happened and was beating her head against the wall and tearing out her hair, cursing herself for having left her girl alone for an hour. She cried to God, to the neighbors, to everyone to help her. But now it was in the hands of the government—and what Jew has ever won against the government?

"The guards took Tahra and Suleika to the Caid's court. Tahra swore that Suleika had said the words and later recanted. Suleika said, 'I was born a Jew, I'll die a Jew.' The Caid took one look at Suleika's beauty and immediately thought of the Sultan in Fez. The Sultan had a harem of at least four hundred women, and it was known that he had quite a few Jewish women. If the Caid sent this beautiful girl to him, he might get a promotion and a bonus. Suleika was found guilty and thrown in the dungeon. The Caid sent word of the beautiful Jewess he held. Soon the word came back from the Royal Palace: Bring the lapsed convert to Fez.

"Guards took her to Fez and straight to the palace. The

women in the harem bathed and dressed her in silks, velvets, satins, and loaded her with jewelry. The Sultan sent for her. A handsome and charming man, he saw this beauty kneeling before him, eyes lowered, and knew he had to have her. All his four hundred women disappeared from his mind as if they had never existed. He wanted only this one: young, innocent, and the most beautiful creature he had ever seen in his life. He fell in love the way he never had before. He promised her riches and power. She could be the head of his harem. He ordered the former Jewesses in his harem who had converted to Islam to speak to her. 'Our life is good,' they told her. 'Before, we worked like slaves, we were treated like dirt, the men in our families sold us to rich husbands. Now we have plenty to eat, lovely clothes, we are happy and treated well. Why continue to struggle as a Jew in an Arab land? Join us.'

"She listened to them and then told the Sultan, 'If you were to suddenly call yourself a Jew, do you think it would make any difference to your God? Wouldn't He still recognize you as a Muslim no matter how you changed your name? And in your heart, you wouldn't change. You couldn't change. Do you understand that my God is the same? He will always find me because He is in me.'

"The Sultan brought the Grand Rabbi of Fez to speak to her. A famous sage, Rabbi Serfaty, pious and learned. He was a friend of our ancestor, the holy Rabbi Abraham ben Avram. These men were so wise and good that white doves flocked around them wherever they went. The Sultan forced

161

Rabbi Serfaty to advise Suleika to convert–in name only, the way the conversos did–in other words, to stay Jewish inside but accept the ruling faith on the outside. 'The Sultan is a tolerant ruler who is kind to the Jews,' the Rabbi told Suleika, knowing that the Sultan hid behind a curtain in the room and listened. 'He will not force you to believe what you don't believe. All he asks is that you say the words so that his people will be satisfied. You know, Suleika,' he lowered his voice, 'I walked to the palace from the mellah, and there are crowds gathered outside at the Bab-Dekaken, screaming for your death. They call the Sultan weak because he hasn't killed you yet. Today a man murdered a pregnant Jewish woman, ripped out her fetus, and threw it at the Palace door. The Sultan is endangering himself for you.'

"Suleika raised her clear eyes to the Rabbi and said, 'Am I dreaming to hear a rabbi, one of our holy men, speak to me this way? Where would our faith be today if at every crisis our leaders spoke as you did? We'd be gone, forgotten. What sort of half-life are you condemning me to? A death-in-life.'

"The rabbi left her with bowed head and wrote about his experience in his journals. 'Today I met an angel,' he wrote, 'and she made me see how much of earth I am.'

"The Sultan didn't know what to do. With each day he loved Suleika more. And gradually she began to return his feelings. How could she resist? 'I love you too much to want you in my harem,' he said. 'I want you for my wife.' He took her to the roof of the Palace. They stood and looked down at the crowd below shouting, 'Death to the Jewish Infidel!'

"Suleika listened, and dread filled her heart. She loved the man at her side–even though he was of another faith– but if this mob should storm the Palace, what could he do to save her? There was no safety, no security in anything but God.

'Say the Formula of Conversion,' he begged her. 'There is no God but Allah, and Mohammed is His Prophet.'

'I can't say what I don't believe. I'll die in my soul.'

'Then die!' he cried in a fury.

"He turned her over to the Grand Caid of Fez. His reputation was that of a cold, stern man, one who believed only in the letter of the law, in hard justice rather than mercy. Many Jews died under his decrees. He'd been waiting to get his hands on this failed convert. He asked her, 'Did you convert to Islam, then recant?'

'No.'

'Muslim witnesses have sworn that you did. A crime punishable by death. Do you have anything to say in your defense?'

'I was born a Jew, I'll die a Jew.'

"He sentenced her to death by public execution in three days. The Sultan roamed the Palace, unable to sleep or eat, wishing he could turn back time but knowing he couldn't. His people would never accept a Jewish woman at his side, and now the wheels of justice had been set in motion.

"Suleika cried in her cell. She was going to die at seventeen. A girl who would never know the love of a husband or the feeling of holding her own child in her arms. Did she

163

think of her mother that last night alone in her cell? Did she ask God for forgiveness for having disobeyed her?

"The guards came for her on the morning of her execution. It was a sunny day in July, three months from the day Tahra had locked the door behind her. The guards unlocked her cell and led her to the square outside the Sultan's palace. Crowds were gathered to watch her die. She kneeled at the block while the executioner touched the back of her neck with the point of his sword. 'The Sultan asked that you be given one last chance to change your mind,' he said. Pinned to the block, she couldn't turn her head, but her voice rang out, 'Shema Israel.'

"Her head flew at least ten feet away."

Mama Ledicia cleared her throat and patted my hand.

"Who was she, Mamy? A saint? A girl in love with the Sultan? An Arab boy? God?"

"I remember when Perla, Mamouche and I went with Sheba to Fez. A rainy, windy day in January. We brought Suleika flowers and a platter of couscous. I remember seeing two Arab women—a mother and daughter—praying at her grave. The daughter couldn't have a baby either. When they left, we walked around the tomb, right next to the famous Rabbi Serfaty's, and lit candles, cried, and prayed. We hugged the white dome of her tomb and kissed it. Then we left, but Sheba wasn't with us. I turned back and saw her holding onto the tomb with both hands, crying as if her heart would break.

"'A'b'nti, a'b'nti,' I said and went to her. She wouldn't let go. It took the three of us to pull her away. All the way home, she cried. When we got back, she told me she was going to have a girl, that Suleika had given her a girl who would be born in October—and you were, on October 1st. What a rich world we live in, t'bark'allah."

I'm shivering, staring at the tiny old woman facing me in the dark. "Tell me how you met Papy."

"Has he been telling you stories again? That old sinner has nothing better to do."

"Is it true that you were almost a bride?"

She smiles. "The women were already singing the bride's song for me. What I hope to sing for you one day." She takes both my hands in hers and sings:

> *Elle sera belle*
> *Ses doigts seront brodés*
> *Apporte le henné du Sous*
> *Pour broder ses mains.*

"They painted me with henna, I was ready to cross the threshold, and then he appeared. Like a burning bush, his hair a red fire blazing around his head. I thought he would burst into flames." She gives her witch's cackle, blesses me on the head and stands. At the door, she turns. "By the way, your father called today. From Israel! He moved there!"

"My father? Are you sure?"

She's gone. I go to the window. Mom? Did you hear that? Has the world turned completely upside down? What's going on? Mysterious hums, barbed wire fences made out of clay,

Dad going to the Unmentionable Place. Did you spin the globe, Dad, and your finger landed on Israel? Was it loneliness? Pain? I don't think I understand anyone or anything. Not Gaby, not my father, definitely not Suleika. I lean out the window. No hum tonight, on my last night in El Kajda, as if she knows I'm coming nearer to her. My last night in my mother's childhood room. My last time looking out of this crazy window at the mimosa tree. I wonder if this house will remember me at all.

I go to the tiny bathroom down the hall to wash away the tears and brush my teeth. I let the water in the sink run ice-cold and splash my face over and over. Suddenly I lift my head and turn. Gaby is in the doorway, watching me. He comes in, shuts the door behind him, grips my head with his hands and lowers his mouth to mine. I try to protest, to move away, but his hands cover my ears, his mouth burns on mine, his body—blocking out all sound, all sensation—except the sweet, sharp heat shooting into me like an arrow. I don't know when I start kissing him back, but I can't tell the difference between his lips and mine, his tongue—

He pulls back, looks straight into my eyes, runs one finger along the line of my jaw. "I'm going to drive you to Fez tomorrow."

## The Repentant King

When the sun's rays fell in the desert
They hugged a great tree,
How much pain I suffer
Since Sol disappeared!

Day and night I spend crying,
Always for you,
And yet of my pain, you know nothing, Ungrateful One,
Of the torments I suffer for you.

Oh! How far destiny brought me
Like a leaf, the wind carried me
Into dark hell! You don't know, Ungrateful One,
The torments I suffer for you.

I will fall silently to the tomb
To seek the lost calm
Kneeling, Ungrateful One, I pray to you:
Remember me. At least, remember me.

Your red lips
The words that drove me mad
Your sweet voice—my music—sighing,
Whispering: Oh yes! Yes!

When you saw me, you felt it, too,
Heat, light, fire—

*You sang it with your voice, your hands,*
There's no more than this: to be joined to you.

*What do riches and honors matter to me?*
*What use is my throne without you?*
*I only wanted to live inside you,*
*And after tasting you, to die.*

*Where is she, who penetrated my heart?*
*Where is she, who tore into my soul?*
*She who changed my life?*
*Tell me, for God's sake, where she is!*

*I wander through the desert, searching for her,*
*My angel, my delicious love*
*I'll never see you again.*
*What good are my hands if they can't touch you?*

*Give me your hands,*
*Give me your love!*
*Don't leave me alone*
*I'm dying, oh God, without you.*

—Suleika's qerida,
sung by the girls
of the judería
of Tetouan

# *the road to fez*

I KNOW HOW TO SEE WITH MY HANDS, and there is-n't one part of her I'm not going to see. She'll be afraid. How many lovers has she had? Three? Four? It doesn't matter. You can see by her eyes they haven't seen where she lives yet. Don't be scared, my cat. We'll be together every step of the way. I almost forgot tenderness. You bring it out in me. I want to make you tremble. Do you know how much I want you? Enough to leave a piece in process at the shed. The barbed wire of my life. One night, little cat. You will never forget it.

So THIS IS DESIRE. To watch his hand on the shifting gears. So odd how the gears are up on the dashboard in this car. A Cit-roën Deux Chevaux, he told me. I didn't notice yesterday but that was because I sat in back, like a kid, behind him and Sylvie. I've graduated to the front seat, grown-up now. He curls and uncurls his fingers, moving them the way he did last night on the sand—was that only last night? I've loved him so long and wanted him to see me. And now he sees me.

169

And I'm terrified he'll see too much. I'm not even sure if what I want from him is sex. Maybe just to hold hands and be friends. The fingers that never stop, that curl and stretch, those beautiful scarred fingers. Imagine them touching you. There. Where you're supposed to scrub and scrub. A wild giggle escapes me. He looks startled, smiles dreamily at me, and returns to the road. What is he dreaming? Probably of how he's going to say good-bye to me at the airport.

I still taste his mouth on mine. I want to keep tracing my lips—as if they hold the answer. I know that when we finally make love, it won't be half as satisfying as my imaginings. I'm not as much a dreamer as everyone thinks. I've made love. With Sun God, I remember the two of us lying on his mattress on the floor, naked, and his cat leaping on my belly and flicking his tongue over my nipples. I almost screamed, and Sun God laughed. The cat watched me with knowing eyes and licked my breast until I couldn't bear it anymore and pushed him off me. Sun God stuck a joint in my mouth and I sat up, coughing. The smell of grass filled the apartment, the sick-sweet smell I always associated with him, with us.

Were we ever not high when we made love? I don't think so. One stormy night—the night I found out Ti had smashed her car into a telephone pole and died instantly—I climbed the stairs to the apartment he shared with three other guys, all avoiding the draft, and fell into his arms. I couldn't cry yet—the way I couldn't with Mom, until months later. My first reaction to pain was always to close my eyes and wish another reality into being: Ti and I exploring each other's bodies in a hushed pink-gray night that had no end.

I told Sun God about Ti, and he said, "Let me take away your pain, baby."

We went in his room, and he tied a rubber hose around my upper arm. His warm wine breath and long, sun-streaked hair tickled my arm. I heard the thread of laughter in his voice: "Don't move, baby. It's such a small vein. I don't want to miss and hurt you." He pricked my arm with the needle. Immediately I felt the heroin enter my blood, travel through my veins, flow through my entire body. Nausea gripped my stomach: it was too rich, too much blood swirling, too foreign and strange an invader in my body. His voice came again, from a great distance: "Sit back and mellow out. You'll get used to it."

Gripping the arms of the chair, I leaned back and watched the room shift. Pink light poured down the walls. Sun God stood in front of me, shadowing the stream of light. He leaned over and kissed me, his mouth filled with harsh smoke he blew inside me. I swallowed, felt a burning in my throat. He pulled me down and lay next to me in a sea garden of roses larger than any I'd ever seen. Effortlessly, my clothes fell off—no buttons, no zippers. That was the first time we made love. When he entered me, the sudden pain shocked me—especially after the numb, sweet high of the heroin. I didn't know it was over, didn't feel him coming inside me, hadn't even thought about protection, or anything. Suddenly he was smiling down at me: "Was it good for you, baby?"

WHO IS SHE DREAMING ABOUT? Not me. The one with the absurd name—Perla told me—Sun King? She misses him now. She's with me but thinking of him. It's starting to hit her now. That we stole like thieves from the house. That she's with her uncle. That the whole adventure can only lead to one thing. That within forty-eight hours she's going to be out of the country and flying home to Daddy. If it doesn't rain—and so far the sky looks clear—we should make it to Casablanca by noon. Stop for lunch and to fill the tank. I'll take her to Mustapha's restaurant. He makes the best bstilla in Casablanca. A nice, leisurely meal. Then back on the road to Rabat, another ninety kilometers. The scenic route, along the ocean. Stop somewhere around Rabat for a bite to eat, maybe a drink. Then turn inland. Another two hours past Khemissat to Meknes. Fez by nine. Ten at the latest. Then what? A hotel. One room. One bed. She won't fight you, she's the one who's been backing you against the wall. One night. I'll be exhausted by then, after driving all day on these shitty roads. Bouncing up and down. I'll revive. Tomorrow I'll take her to the cemetery. We'll pay our respects to sweet Sol. Then—no, before Suleika—the travel agency. Maybe even tonight, check at the hotel desk. Have to get her confirmed on a flight to New York. Tomorrow. If not, we'll have one more night together. I can live with that.

HE SMILES AT ME. Why? Why doesn't he say something? What's he thinking? How I've thrown myself at him for the past month and a half? I want to go home. I want to get out of this car. I don't want him to touch me. He's my uncle, for God's sake. My mother's brother. It's too close, too intimate. I think I'm going to be sick. The car won't stop shaking and bouncing. And it's so tiny I keep falling against his arm. How could I leave Mama Ledicia and Papa Naphtali like that? Sneaking out in the morning with my backpack, Mom's tapestry packed in my suitcase. My legacy. He waited for me outside the mellah gate, leaning against his car, watching me approach. I almost turned back. He looked so remote again, a man carved of marble. Then he roused himself and came toward me, smiling–but without his heart in it. He took the bags from me and said, "S'ba el'her, bella," and kissed me on both cheeks. For a second I thought he might be nervous too, but how could he be? He's probably stolen away with women hundreds of times.

When I reached his car, I looked back and for the first time noticed the Hebrew letters carved on the mellah gate. I couldn't read them but remembered Papy's description of Hebrew waves and pitchforks. A chill went through me, as if the letters were alive, witnesses to my departure. "It's strange," I said, "I feel I'm never coming back here again. That when we leave here, this whole world, the house, the mellah, Papy and Mamy, everyone, will disappear."

He gave me one of his mocking glances. "You don't think it can go on without you?"

"I want it to, I hope it does–but I feel as if it's already disappearing."

In the car he drove silently. I thought about Luc, who had amazed me last night at the Majestic by asking me to go to Paris with him. "I want to show you my city," he said. "I want you to see me there. Someone like–like Gaby stands out here. This is his town. But in Paris, you can see the real me."

You're jealous of Gaby, I thought. You watched us dance on the sand last night, and you sensed something. Just the way Sylvie did in the club, watching me through cutting eyes.

NOTHING CAN BE TOO BAD WHEN YOU HAVE THE SEA at your left, and the promise of the sun ahead. I drive north along the Oualidia, my favorite stretch of road anywhere, the ocean glittering and foaming to my left all the way to Mazagan. At points the sand separating the road from the water is so thin, it's as if we're driving in the ocean. I've never seen sand like ours: gold and thick, with weight and texture. I used to love to roll down sand dunes when I was a kid. My father told me about the ancient art of sand painting. I think that was when I learned that nothing lasts in this world but memory. That we are all particles of what came before. But today, despite everything, I feel new, as if a road I've never taken beckons.

My hands feel better today: the flesh fits the bones again. I stretch my right hand. She's staring straight ahead, little Joan of Arc–light tumbling around her like her curls, a small, brave smile, on her way to the guillotine. It won't be that bad, bella, I swear to you.

IN CASABLANCA, HE TRIES TO BE CHARMING and seductive but the whole thing smacks false. He takes me to a café where the manager calls him by name and looks me up and down in a way that makes me know I'm not the first woman he's brought here. The bstilla–chicken, eggs and walnuts, baked in phyllo dough, sprinkled with sugar and cinnamon–is fine as rice paper, melts on my tongue but gets caught in my throat. I don't like the way he bends over me, attentive and slightly mocking. I don't like the way he calls me bella, or the way he looks at my hair–as if it's not part of me. I'm sick of this heavy mass on my head. When we enter the souk, I see a row of men sitting behind white sheets that display their skills or wares. A scribe with pens, paper, and a beat-up old black typewriter. A doctor surrounded by vials, jars and small bundles of herbs. I stop in front of a sheet with an intriguing assortment of small bottles and tools–from scissors to pliers.

"The barber-dentist," says Gaby.

Barber-dentist? Something in the combination draws me. "Tell him I want him to cut my hair."

I have the momentary satisfaction of seeing Gaby (for the first time) absolutely nonplused. It takes a few minutes to convince him, but he tells the man in Arabic who smiles with a mouthful of pointed, rotting teeth (I hope he is more skillful with hair than with teeth) and gestures for me to sit on the ground before him. He wraps a small white towel around me and squats behind me with scissors that resemble rusted gardening shears.

175

"What exactly do you want him to do?" Gaby asks, looking glum.

"Cut it off. To my chin. It can't be that hard. Will you watch and tell him what to do?"

With a sigh, he squats near the barber who begins chopping at once. Within minutes my hair is a memory, long winding russet-dark snakes coiled around my feet. I touch the back of my neck gingerly. It feels as cool and soft as a child's cheeks. Gaby argues with the barber, takes the scissors from him, and kneels in front of me, tells me to close my eyes, and with diagonal, feathery strokes, cuts the hair around my cheeks, then moves behind me and trims the back. He returns the scissors to the barber and fluffs my hair with his hands, twines curls behind my ears. He pays the barber, and I insist we gather up the fallen mass of hair in a bag the barber gives us. I make him promise to give it to Mani for a new wig. He agrees and helps me shake the stray hairs off my neck and shoulders. The barber has no mirror, so I can only feel with my hands. The hair stops at my nape, curls around my ears, touches my eyebrows. I feel light, as if I'm floating. We stop at a booth where a man sells cosmetics: lipstick stones, rock shampoo, kohl in small jars, silver wands, pumice stones, bags of henna. A row of small round brass mirrors. I pick one up. I can't see my whole face, but what I see feels and looks right. "I think I'm becoming myself," I tell Gaby.

"Must be nice, to look like what you are."

"Do you like it?"

"I don't know yet." But he doesn't take his eyes off me, watches me from every angle, and finally says, "It shows the back of your neck. And the line of your cheek. It suits you."

I IMAGINED US IN BED, HER HAIR CLOAKING US, a fiery tent enclosing us like a veil from the outside world. I wanted to hide inside her hair. Now there's nowhere to hide. Her face is naked, open, so beautiful it makes me ache. She has no idea how beautiful she is.

In the souk she buys me a shaving brush and offers it to me with a smile.

"What else was in that spell?"

"You don't want to know." She leans close and murmurs against my ear, "When you go back, tell Zahra barak al-la'oufik for me."

I don't want to think about going back. My parents, the factory, the uproar. He took off with his niece. What else do you expect from a man who murdered his wife?

She's in front of me, laughing again, and hands me a little boy's undershirt. "Sorry they didn't have your size. Now we're even."

"Are you sure? That's all you took?"

She smiles uncertainly. "The cigarette box?"

"Yes. The cigarette box." The words are thick on my tongue.

She throws her arms around me and says in my ear, "I don't want you to think I stole your soul."

As soon as we leave Casablanca, we start talking and joking. I feel more relaxed, as if cutting my hair freed me. I talk to him about my writing, even discuss a story I began (on Pesach, after his Suleika) about a girl who gets her period on the Exodus, that sandy, irritable, seemingly endless journey. Her mother–of the original generation of Hebrew slaves who escaped from Egypt–is dead. Everyone from that first generation is dead, abandoned in the desert for vultures. Only that ancient wraith Moses remains, cloaked in white, surrounded by a cloud of smoke. When he points his finger at you, flames spark.

There is no one to speak to. The blood pouring from her terrifies her. She has no one to ask. She goes off to a hill to curl up and die. She climbs to the top of the hill and sees a barren, rocky, crater-filled land ahead. A few sparse bushes. She realizes they must have reached the fabled Promised Land. Finally! After so many deaths, so many years, so much heartache and loss. It is not beautiful, not green or welcoming. It's harsh and wild–but she feels a tug in her heart, a need to go farther, to enter the land and make it hers. She starts dancing on the sand, unaware that Moses has ordered the caravan to pack up and return to the desert.

"I've got four possible endings."

"Tell me."

"Moses sees her dance and points his blazing finger at her. 'Unclean!' he roars. Or the slaves return to circling the desert for another forty years or so, without even realizing that they have already reached the Promised Land. Or–no, that one sucks. Or maybe she just climbs over the hill into the Promised Land by herself, while her people stay in the desert–following Old Moses. I hate endings."

"Don't end it," he suggests. "Stop on the hill, before she enters the Promised Land."

"Shouldn't I describe it?"

"My father told me everyone who looked into the Promised Land came back with a different report of what he'd seen. One saw a rich green land, another saw a barren desert. Someone else saw fruit trees, another saw shepherds on a hill."

"As if they're all looking into a pool and seeing their own faces reflected. Like Suleika's story. I feel as if she's humming to get my attention, to make me see her–and understand her. But it's confusing. There are so many Suleikas. Which one is mine? Last night Mama Ledicia told me her version. A sort of moral tale for me, about a bad girl who disobeyed her mother. And my mother's Suleika was a dreary little saint. A goddess of virginity."

He raises an eyebrow. "Goddess of virginity? What's that?"

"What she hoped I'd be."

"And instead look how you turned out. Racing out of your grandparents' house like a thief at dawn. Traveling with that bastard Afriat through Morocco."

"Why do you make it sound so horrible?"

179

"I don't want any illusions. There is no promised land, little cat. Every land is a promise, until you get there and enter. Then you find out it's unclean, and smells bad, and is probably rotting."

"Are you rotting?"

"To the core."

"I like the way you smell."

"Wait till I sweat."

"Why are you doing this?" I ask his profile, his eyes staring ahead at the road. I glimpse palm trees fleeting past, behind his blowing black curls.

"Maybe because I don't want to wake up with a goddess of virginity. Or with a teenager who has a crush on me."

"What do you want?"

He glances at me, then returns to the road. "You, bella. Even without your hair."

"Why? Maybe you see an illusion too."

"Maybe. Do you want me to tell you you're beautiful?"

"No! And stop calling me bella. Makes me sound interchangeable. Am I?"

He glances at me again. "I call you bella because I like the sound of it, it's softer than your name, and because I find you beautiful. And little cat makes me think too much of–things I'd rather not think about."

"Why me?"

"You make me feel–" he pauses, then repeats: "You make me feel."

"I'll disappoint you too."

180

"No. Because I expect nothing. Don't give me that tragic look. You see the world through a veil. Isn't it time you ripped it off?"

I sit over my journal or stare out of the window the rest of the way to Rabat. I'm puzzling over his motives. It's as if he's trying to kill my desire. An immense gray surrounds me. I want to write, to clarify the muddle of thoughts. I steal a look at him, determinedly glaring down the road. I open my journal. On the first page is his name, in ten handwritings, revolving around my name in the center, like petals around the heart of a flower. I blush inside my soul. Turn the pages and skim past self-pitying dirges about my beautiful uncle who won't look at me. I raise my eyes to his hands on the steering wheel. The right hand that doesn't flatten. The burned fingers I didn't see until a few nights ago. Symbols of my blindness.

WHERE I AM NOW IS WHERE YOU ARE, sweet girl. You just don't know it. We're standing on opposite hills—like the enemy soldiers I saw last night—and we've got binoculars focused on each other, but we don't see a fucking thing. I see my little cat, naked now without her hair, the hair I wanted to hide beneath. I saw you riding me like a wave, like a horse, laughing that beautiful laugh of yours, your hair falling over us like a tent. That's my vision. But what do you see? The toy you can't play with. The door you can't open. The forbidden man. Behind a veil. Like a woman. You can imagine anything you want. But I'm here, at your side. Look up from your writing. I'm here. Alive, breathing. A man, bella. Nothing more, nothing less.

"CAN I READ YOU WHAT I JUST WROTE?" When he nods, I begin: "I want to enter you the way I enter a book. The way I enter Suleika's story. The way I always wanted to enter my mother. To understand what was hidden behind the glowing eyes and skin, the long curls I used to wind around my fingers. I wanted to see what she saw when she papered one more layer over the living room walls. I hear the click of her tongue in my ear as I write these words. Am I trying to find Sheba in you? Am I trying to make sense of her death by coming to you? I retraced her voyage, reentered the Old World, looking for her—but all I hear is Suleika's hum, and all I see is you—as if you are both deep in the heart of the book. There must be a way to be in love and still be free."

The echo of my voice trembles between us.

After a while, he says, "I used to think freedom was always being in control."

I don't look at him. We're driving to the end of the world, aren't we? There is no Fez. No Suleika. We've made them all up. Maybe we're the story, ourselves. Two people hurtling down a road to nowhere. I wish I weren't so young. I wish I were like Justine and understood life, and could move through it armed with a camera, a cigar and a cool smile. I wish I knew why he is my holy spark: cold-edged and sharp-pointed, glittering in the dirt. And why I can't let go. The wind outside screams for me to let go.

182

RABAT. WE WALK BY THE MELLAH to the Oued Bou-Regreg. The river is teeming with life, vast and flowing, crowded with women doing the family laundry, kids wading, guys my age smoking and spitting sunflower seeds, old men staring thoughtfully at the water. It reminds me of when the ship docked at Madras, and we went to an enormous muddy yellow river as wide as a small sea, crowded with people—men, women and children—washing, talking, scrubbing clothes, bathing, gossiping, eating, and smoking—as if the river were a street. I breathe in the water, the damp human flesh, the life and movement and pulse. This is my land, but not my land. An exile, ground slipping under me as I stand. They used to call us *the lowest of the low*, make us wear black and go barefoot. Consumed with bitterness, my father rose to his roof and wore only white at home. He needed to transcend the mud and filth of those words. But I saw it differently: once you're called the lowest of the low, there's only one direction you can go, and that's up. Every step takes you higher. Like I told her: no expectations. I am never disappointed by anyone or anything. Only resigned, only tired.

There is nothing to say. She trusts in words. I don't. She can wind them around me, tighten the net, and smile—but I can break through weaves of words. I always have. I let them wash off me. She wants to hear the one word that tells her we're in this together.

She sits on the muddy bank, oblivious to her skirt getting dirty, the kids gathering around staring at her. Her eyes fixed on the people, trying to swallow them. To write about them later. I understand. My hands do the same thing. Imagine having a daughter like her: intelligent, rebellious, beautiful. What a companion. She should have been my daughter. My niece. I close my eyes and open them again. She's not my daughter, thank God for small mercies. Even if I feel old and tired enough to be her grandfather. She's eighteen, I'm thirty. What has happened to me? I feel the mud beneath my shoes pulling me down, like gravity, sucking me into the earth. A heavy weight pushing against my chest, forcing me lower. How did I get this old, this weary? I sit next to her on the dirt bank, light a cigarette, and follow her eyes. River life flows around us–as if we're in a boat. I wish I could lie back, let someone else row for a while, close my eyes, drift.

I TAKE HIS RIGHT HAND IN MINE. He blinks, his eyes the color of water, more gray than green, shining like the arrows of rain that blew on Mom's body when I found her. Sun God wanted to take away my pain. But that wasn't what I wanted. I needed someone to grieve with me, to share my pain, not to be knocked out nearly unconscious. His palm is what I thought it would be: a wrinkled, bleached map of fine lines starting and stopping and crossing each other. The thin wrist, almost delicate. Fingers, ridged and bumpy, but long and expressive, rarely still. Fingertips, stained with jagged bubbling arrows that point down to the wrist. A beautiful hand. The kind of beauty that hurts. I rub his palm and fingers against my forehead, eyes, nose, cheeks, chin. Callused,

184

sandpaper-rough. I take the index finger into my mouth. Taste the tip: bubbled, with a thin strip of withered flesh. The narrow, vulnerable curve between the fingers. The next finger. And the next. Sucking hard, drawing deep on them. The taste of a man's flesh. I touched Sun God everywhere with my mouth, but he was sunny as corn and lemon, nothing like this salt-dark, bittersweet flesh. He watches me steadily, ceaselessly, with eyes that glitter like rain in the dark. I've got nearly his whole hand in my mouth. Wish I could take in the hand to the wrist, and then his arm. I'm wet everywhere, in my hands, my soul, between my legs, every part of me wet and straining to enter him. A child–a little boy, naked from the waist down–suddenly appears at our side, sticks his head between us and peers at me curiously. After a second he runs back where he came from, beyond the edge of my vision. I take Gaby's hand out of my mouth but keep it clasped tightly between both of mine. He leans forward and presses his forehead against mine.

THANK GOD FOR THE LIMITS OF PERCEPTION. That she can't see the pounding of my heart. The fire inside that threatens to burn me alive. Scruples. Small, ugly word. Plans. Always have a back-up plan. Alternatives. Think clearly. Close your eyes. She is the river. I am a boat going down her, through her. The train station is minutes from here. Trains to Fez every hour or so. She breathes like a bird. I always carve slits and holes in my pieces so the spirits can breathe. When I finish a piece, I press my ear against it and listen to the small

185

beating heart. Like the birds we painted that day. She can't remember that. Too long ago. Freedom, I wrote. We're sweating against each other, forehead plastered against forehead, riverglue binding us. A train to Fez. You alone. We'll pull apart, foreheads sucking as if we were attached at birth. Bella, bella—interchangeable. A woman, any woman. One quick rip, like tearing off a bandage, and it's done. She's on a train, and I'm alone again. Back where I started. Free. Alone. Free to—do what? I can't remember. A wet dark smell in you, like the river. If we tip over and tumble in the water, now, float downriver to the source, what will we find? A new land? Fez? The source? Every story begins somewhere. And moves to the point where it's too late to turn back. Don't look for Sheba in me. She's not here. Not in me. Not in you either. Who are we, little cat?

WHY DON'T YOU MOVE? Please show me you're not frozen with remorse. Who was the woman, the one who turned into salt because she looked back? The mellah is salt, your hand tastes like salt. All the tears I've cried over you and will cry over you are here, flowing down this river.

With a jolt, he pulls back from me and gets up. Holds out his hand, almost yanks me to my feet. The car is crowded with us, the river smell, the taste of salt, our sweating bodies, suffocating fear. I clutch the door handle, hesitant to say a single word, that it will darken and change the future. Anything can happen now. Papy saw his bride and leaped in and changed fate. Her destiny, his, the groom's. The children

186

who would have been born. And instead created a new world, one in which Gaby, Sheba, Perla, Elie and Mamouche could spring to life. And Sheba could pray to a dead girl and give birth to me. We drive silently through the city—striped umbrellas shading the entrances to a yellow embassy, pale blue hotel, pink shop, lime-green cafe. A pastel watercolor dream constructed over the city where Saadia Ohana, Haim, Isso and wild Sol lived. He pulls up before a chaotic frenzy of people rushing in all directions. The train station.

Elbows on the steering wheel, he rests his forehead in the heel of his hand. "I'll buy you a ticket to Fez. There are trains all day. You'll get there in about four hours. I'll give you money to take a cab, for food, hotel, whatever you need. Hotel Moussafir is pretty good, and it's right by the train station. You can go see Suleika tomorrow, and then fly home."

"Where? My father's in Israel. I have no one left in the States. I have no home."

"Don't be melodramatic. You have a whole life ahead of you, and I'm not part of it."

"Who's talking about a whole life? I thought we were going away for one night."

"Don't fight me, little cat. I'm trying to do the right thing."

There's so much to say, words bursting to get out. I say nothing, open the door, and get out. He follows me to the trunk. We both reach in at the same time for my suitcase.

"Leave me alone! I can do it myself."

"Let me help you."

I reach in over him, pull out my case, set it on the street.

Turn for my backpack but he's there before me. He slings it over his shoulder, shuts the trunk, and bends for the suitcase. I get it first and grab my backpack from him. He reaches in his jeans pocket, brings out his wallet. "No!" I cry. "I'll be fine. Thanks. For everything." I move toward the train station doors. He says my name. I don't look back. "Allah ma'ek!" he calls. Go with God.

I find the cashier window where I can buy a ticket to Fez, and stand in line behind an enormous kerchiefed woman holding a dead chicken in one hand and a flowered carpet-bag in the other, and two men in white djellabahs, sucking lemons. The line moves slowly. The woman yells at the cashier and shakes the chicken threateningly. One of the lemon-sucking men leers at me, whispers to his friend. They both turn completely around and stare at me while sucking on their lemons, as if they're watching TV. I stare back but I don't see them. Rage clouds my eyes. Without thinking, I whip around with my bags and storm back through the lobby of the station. I'm on the street again, breathing hard. The sky is blue-red, fuzzy as a peach, as if it's already evening, and hours—not minutes—have passed since I went in. I didn't say good-bye. Why did your morality have to kick in now, with me? I stare ahead blindly at the people racing back and forth on the street in front of me. Then I see him. Exactly where I left him. Standing by the trunk of his car. Hands at his sides, looking down at the street. I take a step forward, then another. He looks as if he's caught between the cracks. My childhood fear: one misstep, and I'd sink into the quicksand of Morocco, Suleika, the childhood I'd left behind in the house in the mellah. I take another step. And another. Bumping into people with my suitcase, almost knocking over a kid with my backpack. I drop the suitcase and backpack on the ground, about two feet away from him. He looks up. Eyes clench mine. For a second I'm scared. I know there's no turning back. Without a word, he pulls me against his chest. I feel scorched, slammed against a burning stove. He smells of sweat, tobacco, life. Heat sucks at me, stealing the air.

I BACKTRACK TO A BEACH SOUTH OF RABAT. We throw Sheba's tapestry on the sand, tear off our clothes, and grope for each other. She gets hiccups, then laughs hysterically every time I touch her. "I'm sorry–you, me–I don't know if I can. I'm scared." Heart crashing against my chest, I hold her. The sky ripples with waves. Clouds foam up from the ocean. I try to slow my breathing. Picture a map of Morocco spreading across the sky: cities, rivers, mountain ranges, deserts, natural resources. Where can I take her? Is there any clear, new place left? Unmarked, piercing me like the naked, slender girl in my arms? I sing to her. Songs from childhood, a dirty fisherman's song in Arabic, a French sailor's chant, "Le rêve bleu"–a lullaby Sheba used to sing me. She trembles. I touch her face–luminous, wet with tears–and I kiss them all, drink them up. A star blinks at me through the waves. I bury my face in the hollow of her throat. "Now," she says, "now." I forget grace, finesse, gentleness. I spread her legs with my hips and push inside her. I feel as if I'm going to tear her in half, destroy every part of her, but she lifts her hips and drives right back against me. My body completely covers her. Her hands and legs rail my back.

IN THE DARK, HE'S MINE—the way he was always meant to be. I don't need to see to recognize him. I hear the heat of his desire. I see him with my teeth and bite him with my fingers. I clamp onto his throat, drink from him. Curl around him, a flower stalk, tendrils stretching to my toes. He is the globe of the world I used to spin violently and stop my finger to explore. With each spin of the globe, I discover a new world, a different smell, the deep forever taste of dream. Behind his ear, harsh dark chocolate; on his chest, deep dizzying musk; down his hard belly, salt-pungent foam, as if I'm licking the sea. His eyes are black, all pupil, his face shadows and angles. Steam rises from me, heat and moisture between my breasts and down my belly. Pure animal, I am hungry, ready to devour. I've been waiting a lifetime—longer, longer.

THERE IS CONFUSION IN OUR DARK DANCE. We stop, start somewhere else, stop again, find each other, and cry out. It hurts. Cracks me open somewhere deep inside. An egg running over you. Smear me over you. Glue me to you so I never have to leave, never come out of you, never. I dive from the Djorf into you. Tighten all you want, I'm going into you, past your black line and breaking through. Jammed up tight against your soul. I've been here before, haven't I? I know this place. Home.

190

Later, much later, I let her drive. I need my hands to talk. She wants to know everything. Colors, lights, raw and bare, tear through the car. Estrella sits between us. I tell them both how I set down her burned, charred body and washed the dishes in the sink, my hands swollen, screaming with pain. How the cottage smelled of death so I moved back to my parents' house and sealed my room to keep her out. How I still wake up, arms flailing as I stamp out the flames. Brit puts her arm around Estrella and steers with the other. The night is black. A single star blinks ahead of us. No signs or familiar landmarks. We must have crossed the border without me noticing. Driving inland, down one craggy winding road after another.

*I feel responsible. I was the one who gave her the spell.* I was the one who showed her the secret. *My mother told me you can't predict what happens with the strongest spell. I never thought he'd kidnap her. I prayed she was happy, but I was worried inside, so I went to the saint's hiloula. I wanted to throw a candle in the fire for her and pray to Rabbi Abraham. He was her ancestor after all.*

*I went to the koubba, crowded with pilgrims and beggars. I wasn't the only Arab there. I saw women I knew, and men, and even Christian tourists with their movie cameras filming the ceremony. I bought a box of candles from a crippled old man outside the shrine and went inside. I've never seen so many people in my life! Hundreds of pilgrims dancing and singing around an enormous fire built on charcoal rocks, or kneeling to throw in handfuls of candles, entire cardboard boxes of candles at a time, and watch them erupt and disappear. Their men stood on rocks and chanted from their holy books, while their women did the you-you, and swayed and moaned. I almost fell from my rock: Mama Ledicia! Screaming and praying the loudest, her hands trying to touch the sky.*

*Then it was quiet. Like a spell worked on the crowd. Everyone waited, their faces on fire with faith. I heard a crack of thunder, but the sky was clear. My knees were already shaking.*

*A man screamed, Ha wa ja! Ha wa ja! Dao'dyalna!*

*He's here! the woman next to me yelled. Pray for a miracle!*

*Now! Now! He hears us now! everyone screamed at once.*

*Every part of me shook like a leaf in the wind. These Jews! I've worked for them since I was twelve years old, and they still scare me. I remember my father saying that Allah grants the Jews' prayers because He can't bear to listen to their voices.*

*Candles exploded in the flames and sweat poured down me, but I was still shaking. Now! Now! they were still wailing and moaning.*

*I said, Jewish God, I don't believe in you, but save your daughter. Help her come to no harm. She hurt no one. She was only in love. It all began with love.*

*I threw the whole box of candles in at once.*

*The screams were frenzied now, people twisting and leaping on the rocks around me, as if they were about to throw themselves in the fire. I was crying. I don't know why. Crying and hugging myself and wondering how I was going to get out of here without Mama Ledicia seeing me and cross-examining me, and the crowd trampling me. I could hardly see from my tears. A hand touched my head and whispered in their holy language, lips kissed my forehead. The most beautiful girl I'd ever seen in my life stood on the rock with me. Hugging me. She was warm and smelled sweet as bread baking in the town oven. She smiled. Don't cry, she said in Arabic. Your sister is fine. I'm watching over her.*

*I blinked and she was gone. I was alone on the rock again. But I wasn't shaking or crying anymore. I felt a wonderful peace cover me like a blanket. I wanted to curl up and sleep under the stars. The only thing that worried me was how to tell Mama Ledicia, because I knew I had to tell her what I'd seen.*

—Zahra bnt l'Amima,
oral testimony, April 17, 1969.
In *The Miracle of Hiloula (1968–1972),*
testimonies compiled, edited, and
illustrated by Shlomo Abenhasuera

# travelers' tales

I think I dreamed this place. High, high up a winding mountain road. A leafy grove
surrounded by silver-green, feathery olive trees, guarded by two turbaned men in
white. Gaby laughed when he saw my face, & he reversed the car and parked across
the road from the men who watched us, impassive and still, hands behind their backs.
"It's a refuge for travelers," he said. "They serve soup and tea."

"But—it makes no sense. What if no one comes?"

"They wait."

"But—we haven't passed another car in hours."

"They wait."

We entered and sat at a long table beneath drooping branches. The men served us
spicy harira in ceramic bowls. Suddenly starving, we ate the soup in a rush. Then one of
the men brought us a silver teapot and two tiny gold-painted glasses. Gaby poured the
tea from on high—like Papy—and the smell of fresh mint rose, filling the grove with my
childhood. The air hummed with music—Papy's oud plucking in my ear, Mom singing
as she turned off the light. Gaby leaned over the table and talked to me, but the words
turned to light and all I saw were his eyes—flickering green and yellow, the dark mint
against gold tea. And his smile: a rare gift of complete acceptance. No one will ever
look at me this way again, weave a cloud of leaves and words around me, kiss me with
fingers harsh and sweet as the mint flowering between us. I drank the tea to keep from
crying. I know he doesn't hear the hum, doesn't know what waits outside the grove. I
smell the hunger. I hear the howl.

—Brit's journal, April 3, 1969

TRAVELERS' REPORTS DIFFER as to what they saw
when they entered the Promised Land. Ba-
nanas, oranges and pomegranates growing
wild, or shimmering desert; a place of death, or
one of life. Joseph Lek left Lod Airport on March
27, 1969, and stood on the ground Moses was forbidden and Naphtali Afriat dreamed of at night (sifting the

sand between his fingers). The sky was blue-white, the ground a mixture of sand, pebbles, dust and cracked dirt. Pink petals dangled from dark bushes blooming mysteriously in this dry land. A woman's breasts, Joseph thought, and immediately censored his mind. The sun was brilliant, dazzling, as if he stood in the Sahara, with no place to hide. Buses, taxis, cars and motorbikes expelled clouds of fumes. Black-hatted, side-curled Orthodox Jews walked in a row past him, saying "God be praised," in answer to every question. Girls more beautiful than any he'd seen strutted in khaki miniskirts and Israeli Army epaulets. A mother welcomed home her son, a woman her husband. The old wept over the young, young over the old. Slim dark-eyed men cruising the area clicked their tongues when they saw a pretty girl, with exactly the same mocking, slightly exasperated intonation as Sheba. It made him stop still in shock, as if she were here somewhere waiting for him. Dust, flowers, car fumes, shouts, whistles, clicks. He removed his sunglasses and squinted in the almost unbearable glare.

AFTER MIDNIGHT ON FRIDAY, APRIL 4, 1969, two travelers entered the Imperial City of Fez in a desperate state. We Fassis are used to voyagers coming to us from distant places with fierce desert eyes: our city is a Mecca for seekers. We believe everything can be found here—from Koranic wisdom to skilled artisans to a refinement and delicacy unparalleled anywhere else in Morocco. And of course we have learned

195

the secret of stopping time. Enter Fez el-Bali and walk through the medina, virtually unchanged since the last century. At least 9,412 lanes, alleys, and streets, by my nephew's count.

"Fez sings in my veins," wrote the noted world traveler Constantine Levinas in 1927. "She is blood and sunlight, rose and saffron, the chanting of twilight birds, the end of time and the beginning of time. She is the moon with her white hypnotic craters, each one a reflected prayer, and she is the moon's other face, dark and still, porous and alone as sleep. She is fire eaters and dancers, scourge and bottomless pleasure, blessings of milk, dried dates, olives, figs. She is a world rolled from carpets, burnished gold and copper. She is my heart, which is wall, house, nail-studded doors. A city of guests in djellabahs bearing thola drums and the force of ritual, the air pressed into metal with mallets and castanets. Frenzy of desire and pool of contentment. And there, through the arched doorway: cushions, carpets and pillows. Fez is a river of green, green tea, a sleeping goddess, mistress of the netherworld with enchanting eyes and camel's feet. She is the sum of sacrificial tears that flow beneath the floorboards and the streets, the prophets that dwell in the water, singing, dead and alive, in my arms, my eyes, my blood, my sex, my faith. Let them, I pray, be endless. Let them sing forever. Let them, I pray. Let them."

This was the Fez our love-dazed travelers experienced on April 6th, two days after their arrival. For two days they stayed closed in what I call—with pardonable pride, I hope—

the sweetest hotel in Fez. When they found their way to me, I knew they were special indeed. My hotel is not a four-star establishment, nor is it a lowly one-star. Stars are not to be measured. Although we are in the medina, we are not immediately visible. Your eye can pass right over us. We don't advertise our location. Here is a clue: look for the archway shaped like a great keyhole, next to the turquoise café. But be careful: it's so easy to paint over us, and then we disappear until the next full moon. If you are interested—and you seem to be—here is a quick rundown of our features. The hotel is small: two stories, seven rooms that surround an inner courtyard. The hand-cut intricate mosaics decorating the courtyard are one of the foremost examples of the art of zellij, designed by the fourteenth-century zlayiyyah, master of his craft, Driss Kandisha. In the center of the green, purple, and gold trompe l'oeil geometric designs and configurations is a jasmine tree that drips perfume, one drop at a time, over the gurgling blue fountain. Each room, overlooking the courtyard with its individual balcony or terrace, is painted a single different color. No artwork hangs on the walls: serenity and stillness are the keys to running a superior establishment.

Our two travelers are in the blue room. I put them there because their eyes reminded me of one of my favorite clients, Matisse. After his stay in the blue room, he wrote me the following note: "Cher Rabi, If you come to Morocco for a week, you'll write words; for a month, you'll write phrases; for a year, you'll write a book.... Longer than that, you won't be able to write at all!" Matisse burned for colors; the travelers' eyes burned for each other. I gave them the key and sent them up the winding stairs with our lovers' basket: pale hard cheese they break off with their fingers, flat brown bread, black cherries and grapes they can feed each other, a bottle of wine. The blue room is small and square. A large bed, covered with a hand-woven deep blue tapestry. Private bath, with an antique claw-footed tub I spirited away from the Dar el-Makhzen. The Sultan's favorite had it sent from England in the last century; she preferred a private bath to the communal hammam. Slatted wood doors, painted turquoise, open to the balcony. There is also the roof, from which you can read the moon and see Fez, past and present, unwind its threads around you. But that is another story, for another time. Next time you are in the medina, come find us. Our promise is inscribed in the tiles that border the entrance: we wait for you at the crossroads where moon crosses sun and gives birth to a star.

SULEIKA ENTERED FEZ ON JUNE 25, 1834, tied to a mule, surrounded by guards. She wore a white haïk, coarse and filthy from dirt and sandstorms. The voyage from Tangiers had taken six days. Legend has it that the guards fed her once a day, in the evening. They unstrapped her from the mule and watched her crawl to a bowl of food or liquid to lap it up with her tongue. Legend also insists that the guards were not permitted to speak to her, and she could not speak to them. This was true. In the day the voyage was deadly silent, leaving the girl with too much time to dread what was coming, to search for God in the sky—or in the visions that appeared more and more frequently behind her eyes. But in the dark, when all the guards except one slept and left her, still bound, on the ground, a young man, disguised as one of them, crept to her side, and they talked through the night—under the eyes of the sleepless, watchful officer, his curved scimitar in hand.

Issachar reminded her of the time he'd taken her to see the farce, "l'Aulularia," in the Grand Socco, in which one of the actors wore an enormous wood phallus, jerked it up and down violently, and acted the buffoon while the audience shrieked with laughter. This was called Playing the Jew. After the performance, Isso took his sister's hand in his and ran to the ocean. They stood on the sand and stared at Gibraltar. "Beyond Gibraltar is Spain," he told her. "We'll go there first."

"We left there to come here."

"Torquemada is gone now. The Inquisition is over. Anyway we won't stay in Spain. We'll move into Europe. Somewhere else. Somewhere I will never have to play the Jew again."

Staring at the silver scales of sea and sun, she pictured the fig tree whose roots spread under the ground of their courtyard to her friend Tahra's courtyard next door. The heavy leaves drooped over both sides of the wall that separated their houses. Both she and Tahra had shimmied up the tree to pick ripe green figs, split them open, and suck the juice, smiling at each other through the leaves.

"There must be another way to live," said Isso. When he came home from work, the first thing he did—in silent ferocious ritual—was to tear off the black djellabah and put on one of spotless white. The second thing, even while their mother called to him, "Leave the lazy slut, she's already asleep!"—was to climb the stairs to the roof. Her chest tightened every time he appeared. Tall and dark, in his blinding white djellabah, smiling at her with soft black eyes. Poor as he was, he always brought her a treat—as if she were a child, when she was already seventeen to his twenty-four. Today it was an orange. The day before, mahjoun. And the day before, two plump dates. But no treat until he examined her back. She lay on her stomach on the floor while he lifted her dress and stared at the pattern on her back. She'd never seen it, but she twisted around every day and stretched her fingers to touch and know it. Lines that crossed each other like the thatched roofs of the booths at the Socco. But the stalks were pale green while the diamonds on her back glittered like black-red jewels. She picked and scratched at the crust. Blood was more black than red. Her mother never gave it much of a chance to dry and scab. Instead she layered the diamonds over each other. Embroidering her back the way women embroidered their hands with lines of henna. "We'll marry you quickly so he won't see your back until it's too late," she said. "You won't be so beautiful then, will you?"

Isso's silence when he stared at her back always frightened her. She knew it covered a rage so profound and limit-

200

less that if this gentle man let go, he could destroy the entire house with his hands. After a while, his voice came—soft and deep as his eyes: "She got you bad today." He squatted next to her and began rubbing olive oil in the wounds. Every part of her ached, every bone, every muscle.

"Why—does—she—hate—me?"

"She doesn't—I don't know why. You're everything she's not. Beautiful. Young."

Her breath returned. And her reason. "I won't always be beautiful. Or young. It must be more. I'm her daughter. Her blood. I think she wants to kill me. She says my face is a djinn's curse."

He laughed at that, but it was with despair, as his hands rubbed gently, so gently, around the raw flaming sores. "You are the sun," he said, "never forget that. My Suleika, my little sun."

"She wants me to marry. A widower with six children."

"No."

"What do you mean no? How can I stop her? You can't stop her from beating me. No one can. I think I'll just run away myself and do something. Maybe marrying the widower will be a start. At least I'll get out of here."

"I have a plan," he told her. "I'm saving money to book passage on a boat to Spain. I know a captain, and he's agreed to take us. Tomorrow I'll take you to meet him. If anything happens to me, go to him."

But Isso's tomorrow never came. Instead came the bewilderment of events spinning into frantic motion, with the harsh implacability of the Biblical world, impossible to halt or alter. Her mother was in one of her inexplicable rages again, chasing her through the house with a donkey tail attached to a broomstick. Suleika ran outside, looked around in a panic, and suddenly Tahra was there, beckoning, her door open. It took an instant. Less. To cross the threshold she'd never crossed before. Tahra's door slammed behind her, and she found herself on the other side of the mirror, the other side of the fig tree. The furniture was arranged differently, but the house smelled the same: fresh sharp ksboor, cumin, preserved lemon, orange syrup, mint for the tea. Tahra said, "You'll be my sister. The most beautiful sister in the world. My brother has been away, and he's dying to meet you. . . ."

Now in the dark Isso lay on his side next to her and whispered, "We'll escape when we get to Fez. They can't hold us."

She let him talk, the sound of his voice always soothing. But her visions had begun, and she no longer believed in escape. She couldn't put into words what she glimpsed yet. It emerged slowly, in fragments, like the black-red diamonds on her back.

He told her a story to pass the time, to make her forget. Because the night guard loved tales, he allowed Isso to speak, sat back and listened.

"There was a princess who loved the sun and always faced it like a flower. She sat in her garden under her walnut tree and dreamed of a world in which people were good, and every soul glowed with truth. Her father had taught her to

202

read, so she spent many hours lost in tales of faraway kingdoms and runaway princesses and powerful sorcerers.

"Revolution came to her land. Warriors marched through the kingdom, killing everyone. They murdered her parents and held her prisoner in the palace. Although the new ruler pretended to be kind to her, he only wanted to get rid of her. So he arranged a marriage with the notorious King of the Night. Everyone knew he was a djinn disguised as a human, who ruled djnoun, little people, and evil spirits underground in his ice kingdom.

"She refused, so the guards beat and tortured her, then locked her in a dungeon cell. They told her that they would not feed her or free her until she agreed to marry the King of the Night. Left alone in her tiny cell, she started to cry. Nothing remained of the world she had known, the world of her dreams. She heard a sound and looked up. Her father smiled at her through the bars of her cell. 'I thought they killed you!' she cried.

"Silently, he pushed a white and gold book through the bars, then disappeared. She sat on the cold ground in the dark, but when she opened the book, light burst free from its pages, illuminating the letters. She read the story of a young man who worked in the gardens of the brutal queen of his land. She was a savage murderess who had forced the entire kingdom to worship her god: a pig. The diamond pig sat on his marble pedestal in the courtyard of her palace, surrounded by a grove of walnut trees. It was the young man's job to keep the walnut garden flowering around the pig god.

"But at night he went to his small room, closed the black curtains, and brought out the books his father had left him. The books of mystical wisdom taught him that the true God cannot be touched or seen. He studied the letters. They rose from the ancient pages and took life in the room. He lived, breathed, ate the letters. Wherever he looked, he saw only his God, felt only God, heard only God's voice, until his God was absorbed into his very flesh. He had to wrench himself from this world to reenter the courtyard.

"A maid worked at his side in the gardens. Her job was to polish the statue of a pig. They never spoke. One day he gathered the walnuts that had fallen to the ground. He picked up one that was still green and took it to his room to watch it ripen and see if he could understand the secret of the nut. That night he heard a knock on his door. In terror, he opened it. The maid lifted her veil. Her black eyes stared directly at him. He wanted to touch her because God was in her.

"At that moment the Queen passed on her way to kneel before her pig. She saw the young man and the maid in the doorway. In a jealous fury, she pushed past them, entered the room, and saw the forbidden books. She ordered the young man imprisoned at once, and the maid killed. He was thrown into a dungeon and sentenced to death the following morning. In his cell, he looked at the walnut shell, still green, too soft to crack open. But on the ground he found bits of limestone. He scratched on the wall with the limestone and drew a boat. He touched the boat and the cell wall melted. He sailed away.

"The princess looked up from the gold and white book. Her cell danced with light, the letters filling the dark like little suns, illuminating every corner. On the ground she saw limestone rocks. She picked one up and went to the back wall of the cell and drew a boat. It glimmered and shook on the wall, as if it was already being hit by sea winds. She drew a sail, then dropped the limestone, pressed her hand hard against the boat, and closed her eyes. She sailed away on the boat through wild seas, a tempest rocking the boat. Waves and wind pushed the boat to a desolate island. She saw a huge stone staircase that descended into the ground.

"She climbed down and found herself in an underground kingdom where silver light reflected walls of rock and ice. As she walked, she came to a great hall lit with torches, crowded with people chanting and shouting. A vast table was being set with black dishes and goblets. Servants were everywhere, polishing enormous ebony candlesticks and chairs of black glass. She walked through one cavern after another, each darker and narrower than the one before. Everywhere she went, swords of ice sprouted from the ceiling and the ground, as if they strained to meet. She squeezed her way between the ice spears and stopped in front of a waterfall. The water streamed down rocks and through crevices like black tears that froze before they reached the ground. A scroll, coarse and yellow, jutted from the black ice. She leaned over, pulled it out, and tried to unroll it, but it remained tightly sealed.

"She carried the scroll with her until she came to a vast

gray room with two thrones carved from mountains of rock, each flanked by two gigantic ice horses. A man wearing a black mask and dressed in a gold caftan held out his hand to her. 'You are my bride,' he said. 'I am the King of the Night.'"

I HAVE COME TO THE HEART, THINKS GABY, of the heart of my heart. A new country. I don't remember this hotel, café, street of blue torches. I have been in this city a thousand times, I have never been here. I say words I must have said before, but they blister my tongue and ache between my teeth until I utter them, raw and unformed: a new language. I give her everything, hold back nothing: there is nothing to hold back. How could I have traveled around the world, slept with so many women that I've lost count, and returned to the source: the girl I held on my lap–my sister's daughter, my blood–when I was still a kid myself? As if the traveling and voyages were a circle to lead me back to where it all began. Were you warning me, Sheba? Did you know I was the one in danger? You took her from me, but she found me–and now, sweet Sheba, tell me where to find the strength to let her go. I hear you rustling past at night, hovering over us. I'm lost, Sheba. A man in pieces, held together by riverglue and her.

THE BLUE WALLS ARE COOL. Wood slats send blue-slitted shadows over the walls and floor, the bed, their bodies. The entire room hums with their electricity, bed and walls vi-

brate. They caress each other and speak their language between the bars of light. Her nut-honey sex tastes like wild-
plucked carob, so sensitive to his tongue she screams and almost pulls out his hair. She explores his silk-hard erection
with eyes, mouth, fingers, rubbing it over her face and body,
until he sees stars in the room, stars dancing over her flesh,
stars on her nipples and between her lips.

I AM ON THE KNIFE-SHARP EDGE OF DREAM and waking,
thinks Brit. They climb to the roof and see the city slice open
before them. Clusters of streets, honeycomb houses, orange
trees blooming in sunken gardens. Minarets and mosques
and mellah and medina and Ville Nouvelle, layer upon layer,
overlapping, dripping into each other. My grandmother Alice runs down an alley of bleached bones leading to the
prison where Suleika grips the bars. Gaby and I ride the
horse on my mother's tapestry, searching for a hole in the
walled city, a gate to the sea, a way out of the tangled red and
blue threads. I will find it. I swear I will.

"THE FIRST IMPRESSION IS THAT OF AN IMMENSE CITY fallen
into decrepitude and slowly decaying," wrote Edmondo De
Amicis, who arrived in Fez in the late 1880s. "Tall houses,
which seemed formed of houses piled one upon the other,
all falling to pieces, cracked from roof to base, propped up
on every side, with no opening save some loophole in the
shape of a cross; long stretches of street, flanked by two

high bare walls like the walls of a fortress; streets running uphill and down, encumbered with stones and the ruins of fallen buildings, twisting and turning at every thirty paces; every now and then a long covered passage, dark as a cellar, where you have to feel your way; blind alleys, recesses, dens full of bones, dead animals, and heaps of putrid matter; the whole steeped in a dim and melancholy twilight. In some places the ground is so broken, the dust so thick, the smell so horrible, the flies so numerous, that we have to stop to take breath.... To the right and left are crowded bazaars; inn courtyards encumbered with merchandise; doors of mosques through which we catch a glimpse of arcades and figures prostrate in prayer.... The air is impregnated with an acute and mingled odour of aloes, spices, incense and kif.... We cross, jostled by the crowd, the cloth bazaar, that of slippers, that of earthenware, that of metal ornaments, which altogether form a labyrinth of alleys roofed with canes and branches of trees."

THE OLD CITY HASN'T CHANGED, Justine Mendes thinks as she sets down De Amici's *Morocco: Its People and Places* in a bookstore on the Boulevard Mohammed V. But more ancient than the medina and more locked in tradition is the fact that Fez always has been and probably always will be a man's city. She thinks of the photographs she's already taken here: men studying Koran, leaving their babouches at entrances to mosques to pray, playing chess and backgammon at cafés, smoking on the street. Men, everywhere men. Where are the women of this city? Men's faces are flat, boring, they don't have the infinite depth and subtlety of a woman's face. Only a woman knows that the true secret is the one that reveals its face: the more you stare at it–open, before you–the more it fascinates and draws you deeper. Everything is there, and nothing. Men hide a sla behind a boys' gymnasium, a mellah behind a medina, a palace behind a peeling hovel door, a woman behind a veil. As if there's some great trick to scratching away the layers of masks. As if the greatest secret isn't the one in a woman's eyes.

She leaves the bookstore and ventures outside to continue photographing her series: *Land of the Door*. It is May 9th, 1969, two weeks after Brit has flown to Israel to join her father, and Gaby has disappeared for parts unknown. The memory of the lovers lingers in the voluptuous scent of cinnamon, dark spices and oranges that lures Justine deeper into Fez el-Bali. Something about Brit's eyes, laughing and guarded at the same time, her smile unfurling like a flower, pierces her with regret.

Deep in the heart of the medina, she stops at a turquoise café, its open door painted deep blue, decorated with calligraphy and stars, protected by a carved hand of Fatima. The mustached proprietor, outlined in black like a stained glass figure, rises from the back to come and greet her. A sudden panic seizes her, and she runs. The next day she tries to find the street, the café, the door. And the day after that.

WHEN BRIT AND GABY VENTURE OUTSIDE THE HOTEL, they wear dark glasses (provided by the proprietor of the hotel) to shield their eyes. They hold hands tightly and stand inordinately long at stoplights while they decide which way to turn. The city speeds past them, traffic roars in their ears, impatient people jostle them and turn back. Two travelers in dark glasses, holding hands, standing very very still on a corner in the Ville Nouvelle. The light changes two times, three times, and still they stand. Sometimes they forget they are no longer in the blue room, and they fall into each other with such raw need, it makes passersby nervous. Especially here, in the stern city of Fez, where the moral tone of the country is dictated. A man cloaked in white pokes a stick at them. A mother covers her child's eyes. Teenagers jeer with their jealous mouths.

The lovers see none of it. They move on, hand in hand, to the next corner. The Fez they perceive is an island in the sea. All around them are sharks, stinging poisonous jellyfish, signs that say: KEEP OUT. They are swimming toward the island, not sure which one of them is leading, which one following. They stop again, take off their glasses, and stare at each other. "We don't have much time," he whispers urgently.

"I'm never leaving Fez," she promises.

"I'm never leaving you." He kisses her shorn hair—the dark red-burnt gold of a mountain sheep—and her eyes and nose and mouth and throat—while car horns honk and the muezzin cries, "Allah Akbar!" and a cab screeches to a halt, almost hitting them. The driver leans out his window and curses them. She's on the airplane already. He's kissing her, holding her here, motionless (though vibrating) in his arms, but she's staring down at him from the plane window, already retreating, receding in the white-blue sky.

Isso continued his tale the last night before they entered Fez. While the guard watched, he fed his sister dark, cracked olives from the silver-green trees they'd passed. Bitter, hard, they went down like small stones. She was so weak she couldn't sit up without his help. He crouched over her on the ground and held his water pouch to her cracked lips. She sipped and almost fell against him. He sat, put his arm around her, let her lean against him.

"Who will you marry when I'm gone?" she said softly.

"No one. I'll never marry."

"You will marry. You've been too busy worrying about me to see other women. But when I'm gone, you'll be free to open your eyes."

"There are no other women. There is only you."

"Finish the story," said the guard.

"The princess ran from the King of the Night, but his people caught her and dragged her back. They pushed her onto the throne next to his and placed a crown of ice on her head. After the wedding ceremony, servants prepared her for the wedding night. As they draped her in a gold dress encrusted with jewels, they warned her: 'Whatever you do, don't take off his mask. No one can look directly into the face of evil. The two brides before you tried to see what he hid behind the mask. They are buried even deeper underground than we are.'

"They pushed her into the bridal chamber and shut the door. The King lay completely still on a vast stone bed covered with a sheet of black silk that rippled like the night sky. She advanced with a lantern and peered into his face. His eyes were closed. He slept. The mask was not black but ashen-gray. She touched lightly. It pulsed with warmth, like human flesh. She traced deep-set eyes, a straight nose, a well-shaped mouth. He breathed in ragged gasps, a wounded animal. Despite her fear, she felt compassion for him. What sort of creature was he?

"With the gold light flickering over the face that turned paler the longer she stared, she knew that the answer to his secret was not in his face. She had learned that the face can always lie, but the soul is bound to truth, no matter how grim or frightening. Was he so evil that no human could come close to him and survive? If I too have to die, she thought, then at least let me die knowing the truth.

"She set down the lantern and, with unsteady fingers, began to unbutton the hundred tiny buttons of his ornate gold caftan. She started at his throat, and as she opened each button, gold traces of light sparked on her fingers, as if each button held its own secret. Gently, she pulled open the

212

caftan and stared. A staircase descended into his chest.

"Grabbing the scroll, she climbed down the jagged, uneven stairs, steep as a cliff of rock. She found herself in a town square. The stench of poisonous fumes and rotting fruit made her reel. Torn pages and broken bindings floated past in puddles of dirty water. A donkey tail, hard and stiff, slapped her cheek. She cried out, but no one heard her above the shouts. Red birds shrieked and clawed at her face and arms. People glistened with sweat, slid off each other in the narrow street. She grabbed onto something to keep her balance. The head of a dwarf. He laughed up at her, lifted her hand from his white shaved skull, and leaned over, exposing a hole from which green and black serpents escaped, hissing, to the street.

"The dwarf saw the scroll under her arm and reached for it with a shout. She ran. The crowd chased her. She raced down an alley past barefoot, empty-eyed beggars who clung to her with hands like hooks. She joined a circle of smiling fat men seated around an enormous brass water pipe. Each man sucked on a mouthpiece that wound and slithered from the pipe like an octopus tentacle. She smoked with them until she forgot the serpents and the burning books.

"After a while, leaving the scroll behind, she wandered into a dance. Boys beat on drums with their hands. Young men in green robes danced. She moved with them, arms raised above her head. Eyes closed, she grabbed a red bird. Still dancing, she opened her eyes and stared at the screeching fiery bird. Blood dripped down her arms and hands.

"An old man offered her mahia. She drank until her tongue curled like a flame. She danced with him, then lay on the ground and bore his children. One after another, they escaped from her womb, snarling and hissing like the snakes from the shaven dwarf's head. The infants were born sleepy and diseased, with pointed scaly scalps and filmy white eyes.

"She returned to the dance but felt eyes on her. A man with gray eyes, the color of clouds and tears, watched her. Under his pitiless gaze, she remembered the scroll. With a cry, she ran back to the water pipe street. A fire blazed in the center of the street, releasing billows of thick black smoke. As she looked more closely, she saw that the people were burning a mountain of books. Men and women held out their hands to the fire and breathed deeply as if they smelled flowers. As she watched in horror, the dwarf threw in the scroll. The letters writhed and clawed their way up from the flames, screaming in pain as they whirled madly, charred insects, and then, cracked in the flames. She opened her mouth to scream but no sound came out.

"Suddenly a staircase appeared, rising from the burning scroll. At the top of the winding stairs, the cloud-eyed man waited for her, hand outstretched. She leaped into the flames and felt her flesh shrivel and sizzle, like the letters in the scroll. But she kept running up the stairs. Mossy and slippery, turning in an ever-narrowing spiral, hundreds of tiny steps like the buttons of her husband's caftan. Finally she glimpsed light above. 'Let me out!' she cried. 'Please let me out!'

214

"His cloud eyes blinked as if to hold back rain. 'What would it take for me to set you free? Now that I've tasted light, how can I let you go?'

"Heat shimmered between them as she reached up to him. He knew that he had to release her from his soul. But she burned inside him like desert sun, leaving no part of him untouched. One more moment, he begged his God, and all the gods of the universe. Just one more moment, let me hold her inside me, so I will always remember the taste of desire.

"'Who are you?' she asked. 'Why is your soul filled with so many horrors?'

'I am a Jew. God's witness. The world's demon.'

'She looked at his sad, gentle face, and said, 'Touch my hand. You're not alone anymore.'

'Light blazed through him as if he had swallowed fire, and he reached for her.'"

After a long silence, the guard stirred. "Is that the ending?"

"The end can't be told yet."

"Why not, you donkey son of a whore?" he demanded. "What about the secret of the walnut?"

"What happens when they touch?"

Isso looked at his sister: she held all the gold of the sun in her hands. "The moon burns red and the sun freezes black. Cities crumble, and men forget how to walk. People emerge from caves and look at the world with eyes that see for the first time."

She leaned forward, stared at him intently. Eyes wide, lips parted. See me, he whispered silently, see me now, little sun, before it's too late and we've been swallowed by the earth.

She stared into his eyes and saw the brother who told her tales: a refuge to which she could retreat when her life was too killing and brutal. And behind him the one who fed her and rubbed oil on her bruises with fingers that moved like a soft mouth over her tender, wounded flesh. A man with tortured eyes. Isso's eyes. She stared at him and stared through him, and he knew she finally understood. She cried out, and the guard pulled them apart.

That long, long night Isso and Suleika lay on the ground, unable to touch or even to talk, but neither slept: they wept and watched for each other under the caressing moon, and when the sun rose and burst into flames, their fingers were traced with gold.

Brit and Gaby go to Fez el-Djdid to the Place des Alaouites. On one side of the square is a tired flea market: old appliances, used clothes, a broken chair toppling on three legs. Touched by the long fingers of the afternoon sun, the polished brass doors of the Dar el-Makhzen, the Sultan's Palace, gleam. Next to the palace is the entrance to the mellah, with its incongruous ornate iron-grilled balconies and doors, the kind that Brit imagines in the French quarter of

New Orleans. Ahead of them is the Jewish cemetery–more Hebrew letters, curving and wailing in black iron to the sky. At the gates, beggars shriek like seagulls. Gaby hands them coins, and they reach toward him with harsh cries.

The cemetery caretaker leaves his small white office, gives them each a stubby white candle, and leads them to Suleika's tomb. Tall and stooped, in shapeless shirt and trousers, he looks elongated, as if he stepped from an El Greco painting. Tombs are tiny, planted nearly on top of each other. Brit pictures them in moonlight: petrified animals poised to strike. Gaby sees Estrella's tomb in the Jewish cemetery of El Kajda, separated from the other family tombs because she was a suicide. They walk with heavy steps, trying to hold onto each other down a narrow, twisting path, half-hidden by tall weeds.

"Here she is!" announces the caretaker.

Here she is? Suleika, here? Brit stares at the pointed white roof–topped by three small green-domed cupolas–rising about eight feet above the ground. Suleika's tomb looks like a little house, with a black recessed opening into which you duck to light your candles and pray. She walks around the tomb. Stray grasses blow against the side and back. Rabbi Serfaty's grave is right next to Suleika's. The Serfaty clan seems to be encroaching on Suleika's territory, spreading so close to her tomb she has to squeeze past. On the side of Suleika's tomb is an inscription painted in spindly black letters, as if a child scrawled the words. The first four lines, shaped in a rainbow arc, are in Hebrew. Underneath is this epigraph in French:

*Ici repose Mlle Solica Hatchouel*

*Née à Tanger en 1817*

*Refusant de rentrer*

*Dans la religion is-*

*lamisme les Arabes*

*L'ont assassinée à Fez*

*en 1834 Arrachée de sa*

*Famille tout le monde*

*Regrette cette enfant*

*Sainte*

(Here rests Mlle Solica Hatchouel, born in Tangiers, in 1817. Refusing to enter the Islamic religion, the Arabs assassinated her in Fez in 1834.
Torn from her family, all the world mourns this
holy child.)

Brit returns to the front of the tomb, where Gaby and the caretaker are having a laconic conversation in Arabic.

"How many of us still in Fez?"

"Maybe a hundred."

"How's life?"

"For the rich, good. For the rest of us—" the caretaker shrugs.

"Many people come here?"

"For Sol ha'Tsadika, yes." He kisses his fingertips. "Arabs and Jews. Especially women praying for a baby. They bring her couscous, money, flowers. Her baraka is still very powerful. At night her tomb glows. When you touch it, your fingers burn. If you see a double rainbow over her tomb, she will answer your prayer. If you and your wife want a baby, you've come to the right place."

Gaby studies the small niches carved in the dome, burned stubs of candles, dead stumps of wishes. Is it possible that his bella is the result of a prayer to a dead girl? That her spirit haunts the cemetery? That Suleika hummed to Brit to lead her here?

The caretaker leans over and tells him, "Your wife has beautiful eyes. They say Suleika's eyes burned through lies. After she died, the Sultan couldn't lift his right arm. He had to beg her forgiveness and rub his arm against the stone of her tomb. That was when the cemetery was in Fez el-Bali. They moved it to Fez el-Djdid about fifty years after her death." He lowers his thin dark face closer to Gaby's. "They say she smelled like fresh, warm bread when they dug her up. Her body was still–flesh."

Gaby looks at the sad eyes, long nose, pointed black goatee. "Why are you here? What's in it for you? You're young. Why hang around the dead?"

"I keep them alive." He holds out his hands, palms up. "I carry them."

Brit turns to Gaby, eyes lit from within, a vision glowing behind her face, and he feels a swift jealousy. The first thought she's had away from him since they arrived in the city, the first vision they haven't shared. "A match?" she asks. "I want to say a prayer."

He hands her one of the white candles, the kind Jews throw in by the boxfull at the hiloula, in two weeks on Lag ba'Omer. Suleika is a female saint, so no hiloula for her. Back in El Kajda, Gaby's father–if he isn't too broken by his son stealing away with his granddaughter–will be preparing for the hiloula of their ancestor, Rabbi Abraham. Because of him, Brit will miss it. The barbaric grandeur, the chanting around a fire, candles erupting in the flames, the shattering cry at midnight: "Ha wa ja! Ha wa ja! Dao'dyalna!" And everyone crying out their prayers at the same instant, begging for miracles, for God to open His ear to us once more– through Rabbi Abraham. Miracles did happen at the hiloula. Skeptic though he was, he'd heard of cases in which the lame walked, the blind saw, the deaf heard. If he were at the hiloula now and Rabbi Abraham looked down at him from the sky, he would throw his candle into the blazing fire and ask him for one miracle: to stop time.

He lights Brit's candle and his, and watches her bend over the recessed niche. What is she praying for? he wonders, jealous again, wanting every part of her. He pushes in next to her and thinks he may as well pray to this poor little girl, like Estrella, a creature born and dead in pain. Who better to pray to? Stop time, he begs her. I'll do anything for you, fight for them to give you your own hiloula, make an annual pilgrimage here, anything. Let the world continue on its race, but without us. Draw a magic circle around us so it will always be now and we'll always be together.

Brit rubs her forehead against the cool stone. She feels nauseated, stomach lurching to her throat and back down. What do you want from me, Suleika? Why the hum? Why the call? But you're not even here, are you? Of course not. You wouldn't stay in a house of dead, when everything in you called out for life. I'm going to be sick, really sick. Was it the cheese this morning? The coffee thick and black as mud?

"What's wrong?"

"Get me out of here. Please. Now."

Gaby drags her down the narrow path—the caretaker crying out in surprise behind them—to the gates where the beggars wait, sharp-eyed and claw-fingered, on the other side of the bars.

Outside in the square, she looks around wildly. "Oh my God. Oh my God." She sinks to the ground, head between her knees.

Isso PUSHED HIS WAY TO THE BARS of Suleika's cell at the Prison Sidi-Fraj. Even at this moment, prison guards surrounding him, furious crowd screaming for the blood of the Jewish whore who had stolen the Sultan's heart, even here and now, he wanted to be strong but couldn't stop himself from asking, "Does he love you? Is it true what they say?"

The look in her eyes made him feel faint. "Him? He doesn't see me. Only you. All my life, only you—" He leaned toward her, as if the wind pushed him, and touched her face between the bars. "Oh Isso, you are the garden I used to dream of, the sun warming me, the moon watching over me—it's all you."

He kissed her, tasting her soft mouth for the first time, against cold iron. They kissed, and he married her, had children with her, loved her the way no one else ever could, the way he knew she needed to be loved. He heard her cry out when he touched her: little cries, like a bird in pain. And together they grew old, and he thanked God for every day and night he spent with her because he knew even a lifetime would not be enough.

After an eternity, she pulled away and he looked at her with soul-dark eyes. "Say the words. Say them and live. Even with him. As long as you stay alive."

"I can't. Not even for you."

"I have to know you're alive. I can't go on if you're not. Say the words, Suleika." He pressed his forehead against hers through the bars.

"Isso, listen. That night, after you told me your tale, I had a vision. It came to me in pieces, but this morning I finally saw it whole. Listen, so you'll know how to find me. Every night I've been building a house on the sand. There are three entrances. One is mine. One is hers. You don't know her yet, but you will. One is yours. The doorways are arched. When you reach your door, you won't need a key: it will spring open. Inside, don't be afraid, even though everything will be buried under layers of sand. Go to the inner tiled courtyard.

There is a garden. In the heart of the garden, you will find a blue door."

THE SQUARE FILLED WITH PEOPLE. Brit saw them clearly. Mountain men, warriors from the Rif, Berbers from the Atlas Mountains, the legendary Blue Men of the Tuareg, nomads from the Sahara. Dancers, sword swallowers, storytellers, heddaoua, snake charmers. Soldiers on horseback brandished swords and rode through the crowd, trying to keep order. One of them rode through her. When she cried out, Gaby tightened his arms around her. "I'm here," he said, "I'm with you," but she couldn't hear him anymore. Women shrieked the you-you: sign of joy, index finger against tongue. Brit's mother did it at rare moments in America, while Brit watched, terrified of the shrieking, inhuman cry that trilled from her mother's throat. Jews emerged from the mellah, barefoot, in black, moving like hunched crows, bounded on all sides—not permitted to meet a Muslim's eyes, to ride a horse, to wear shoes, or any color but black.

She pushed her way through the crowd, Gaby's arm on her shoulder. No one felt her. No one saw her. Screams and cries rose, deafening, and then suddenly, a hush. Expectant. They brought Suleika in on the back of a mule. A long veil covered her face and body. Her legs were strapped to the mule's side. The executioner—whom Brit noticed for the first time: sallow, thick-lipped, with long, narrow eyes—advanced, whistling through the air with a curved scimitar that glittered. He cut the ropes binding her to the mule. Suleika nearly slid off, balanced herself by clinging to the mule's neck for a moment, then stood straight.

She's small, Brit thought with a sudden pang. So small.

The executioner slashed the veil from her face.

Brit caught her breath, along with everyone else in the square. Suleika's hair, a black cloak of raw silk, fell past her waist. Face, a radiant soft dream pressed against black moon. Her beauty–like Gaby's–a promise, yearning and transcendent.

She asked for sarwal.

"You won't need them," the executioner said with a sneer.

She said gently, "Please. So that when my body falls, it won't be stained by strangers' eyes."

He looked into her eyes and shouted, "Sarwal!"

A young Jew moved through the crowd and gave her a large pair of blue trousers. He helped her tie them around her slender waist.

"Water," she said. "To wash my hands and pray."

The executioner rolled his eyes. The crowd rumbled with impatience.

Brit moved closer. There must be a way to stop this, to rewrite the ending to this story. Now that she knew she could walk through people, she moved to the head of the crowd with swift, unhesitating strokes, Gaby's hand on her shoulder. With a suddenness that almost jolted her out of this world, she knew he would never leave her, no matter where she was, no matter what happened, he would always be with her, his hand on her shoulder, steadying her, as he did now, anchoring her to the world in which they both lived.

NAPHTALI AFRIAT STOOD ON HIS ROOF, wind tangling his long white hair, staring at the empty brass cages, reminders of the beauty he'd held captive once, briefly, before releasing it to paint a rainbow in the sky. He closed his eyes and smelled the sea and saw his son with his arm on Brita's shoulder. Should he have interfered in destiny yet again? The stakes had been so high, two souls–like magnets–searching for each other: he'd heard the click when they fastened onto each other years before, on the roof, as they painted the pigeons, and even then he had envisioned the possibilities, problems, checks and checkmates. He saw his son–despite his flaws, still his favorite–lower his face and kiss the back of her neck, and raise brilliant, dazzled eyes–the way he imagined the sun in Israel. And he opened his eyes, not wanting to trespass in their world any longer.

FIERCE DESERT LIGHT SHINES ON THE SQUARE that July day, even though we are in young watery April. People shout and chant as I advance to the front of the crowd, a few feet from Suleika. The executioner carves the air into squares and diamonds. An artist, proud of his work. The screams calm in anticipation. The waited-for release. He lifts the heavy rope of her hair and points the sword into the back of her neck. "In his mercy, our Sultan, the great Moulay Abderrahman, has offered you one last chance. Remain a Jew, and you will die. Say the word, and you will live."

"Say the word!" I scream. "Please Suleika! Listen to me and say the word!"

Head locked in place by the sword embedded in soft flesh, she moves her eyes—and looks at the beautiful man standing next to me, tall and pale, with blueblack hair and eyes. The air shudders between them. He sways, leans against me. I put my arm around him to steady him. Before I can cry out for the executioner to stop, her eyes move to me. Focus and lock. Break through the bars of time. Shatter glass. Blow open the door. Howl like the wind. I hear the sword slash through flesh, bone, tendon, vein. The square pulses. He screams soundlessly at my side. I watch my soul walk through the square and out of the light.

Still gripping his arm, I turn to him. "I saw her. She saw me."

"I know," says Gaby. "I saw her too."

# Glossary

Words are Arabic or Judeo-Arabic unless specified otherwise.

AA'WILI  *Woe is me*

A'B'NTI  *My daughter*

BARAKA  *Mystic power attributed to saints and holy beings*

BARAK ALLA'OUFIK  *Thank-you*

CAID  *Local chief*

CONVERSO (Spanish)  *Also known as 'marrano,' a person who was converted to Catholicism under duress but still considered to have 'tainted' Jewish blood*

DJINN (PL.: DJNOUN)  *Demon, evil spirit*

HA'TZADIKA (Hebrew)  *The holy one, as in Suleika ha'Tzadika (Suleika the Saint)*

HA WA JA! HA WA JA! DAO'DYALNA!  *He's here! The saint is here! Our light is here!*

HEDDAOUA  *Wandering Berber minstrels*

HILOULA (Aramaic)  *Wedding between God and His people, through the sacred intermediary: a saint; traditionally a pilgrimage to the koubba, the saint's shrine, to pray for miracles; held on Lag ba'Omer.*

KSBOOR  *Cilantro*

228

# glossary

LA'BASS *(No problems) How's it going?*

LA'BASS. KUL SHEEB'KHER? *Fine. And you?*

LALLA *'Madam,' also a saint, as in Lalla Suleika*

LE REVE BLEU (French) *The blue dream. Lyrics to the song: Leger, mysterieux/ Comme un oiseau/ S'envolant dans les cieux (Fragile, mysterious/ Like a bird/ Flying away in the sky.)*

L'HAMDOU LILLA *Praise God*

L'TAM *Face-veil, covers nose, mouth and chin*

MAGHREB *'West,' used for Morocco and North African countries.*

MA'NISHTANA HA'LILA HAZEH MI KOL HA'LEILOT? *Pesach song that asks: 'Why is this night different from all other nights?' and offers four ritual answers*

MEDINA *'City,' now used for the original Arab section of a Moroccan town*

MELLAH *Jewish Quarter*

M'SHI'KAPARA *May I be sacrificed for you; give me your pain*

M'SKINA *Poor girl*

OUD *11-string fretless Arab lute*

PESACH *Passover, a Jewish holiday that commemorates the exodus of the Hebrews from Egypt*

S'BA EL'HER *Good morning*

SEDER *Ritual meal on the eve of Pesach, during which Jews all over the world eat foods that honor the memory of their ancestors, and read from the* Haggadah, *a book of prayers and songs*

ZELLIJ *Geometric mosaic tilework used to decorate buildings;* zlayiyyah *one who works in the craft of zellij*

229

# *Acknowledgments*

Ishai, Arielle and Avi: *without you, wings of my heart, there would have been no voyage.*

Danielle Knafo, *sister and dear reader: la vida esta muy y mas extrana;* Jerry and Tricia Knafo, Marcelle Setton: *for ceaseless encouragement, hugs and laughter and great food.*

Susan Ramer: *agent extraordinaire, for your faith, warmth, and constant support.*

Trish Hoard: *my editor, who enthusiastically and tirelessly traveled the road with me over and over until we discovered new paths beneath the old.* And Jack Shoemaker, John McLeod, Heather McLeod and everyone at Counterpoint: *for sharing your honor, integrity, and humor.*

Shirin Neshat: *for graciously lending your haunting image to my words.*

Judy Lasker, Joyce Hinnefeld, Martha Posner, Athena Kildegaard, Alla Toff, Jeffrey (Constantine) Levine, Deborah Keller: *my fezzing friends, for accompaning me under moon and rain, sirocco and snow, no maps – but the mythical city glowing ahead:* que tengan duende. . . *and the memory of the sun – always.*

Larry Silberstein, Chava Weissler, Ilana Voloshin, Larry Fink, dear FRGers, Priscilla Prisms: *friendship and inspiration.*

## *acknowledgements*

Nancy Nordhoff at Hedgebrook, the Corporation of Yaddo, Millay
  Arts Colony, Virginia Center for Creative Arts, Pennsylvania
  Council on the Arts: *for offering time, space and a room of my
  own.*

All the yearning hearts: *who looked into Suleika's story through the
  years and found a metaphor for their own desire–for God,
  truth, beauty, understanding.*

Suleika: *good night, sweet sister: I kiss your lips.*